STOLEN

ALPHA'S CLAIM, BOOK FOUR

ADDISON CAIN

Dear Janu,
Please enjoy this
delicious taste of
Darkness!
♡ Addison Cain

Photography by Wander Aguiar
Artwork by Zakuga
Cover art by Raven Designs

FOREWORD

The Alpha's Claim series would have ended with this book, incomplete, had I not been supported through the fight against my former publisher. I dedicate this book to the Magnificent Seven—a group of amazing authors who stood against a bad actor and fought side by side so we could free our books from an unscrupulous felon.

I dedicate this book to the amazing Intellectual Property attorney who led us to victory, Tynia Watson. Lady, you are wonderful beyond words.

I dedicate this book to the Authors Guild, who has since promised to represent any author who had signed with my former publisher in an effort to get their rights back.

I dedicate this book to every last author who is

still fighting to have their rights returned. I will stand by your side until the end.

1

Bernard Dome

Mid-morning sun reflected off the glass so sharply, even squinting, Brenya's eyes began to water. Gloved hands to the East Sector solar plate, she twisted in her rigging, searching out the perfect angle so light might distort and show hidden danger.

Right there... refraction.

Helmet flush with the damaged pane, she traced over the almost imperceptible feather-like cracks marring the clear amorphous metal.

Routine maintenance scans had misclassified why K73-2554's solar collection was malfunctioning. It was not a wiring issue; the pane was about to shatter. Damage of this nature led to serious ruptures, evacuations of sectors, and the potential death of everyone inside.

Speaking evenly, she catalogued all she'd found to the tech team supporting her climb behind Bernard Dome's glass. "Unit 17C to terminal. Pane K73-2554 is damaged beyond original assessment. The structure is badly cracked and will need replacing once fabrication is complete."

There was a hiss of white noise before her tech's radio communication came through. *"Copy, unit 17C. An urgent status notation has been logged into the repair queue. You are granted clearance to patch while we wait for fabrication. Manufacturing posts a three-hour timeline."*

According to her oxygen reserves, that would give Brenya just under an hour to complete install. It would be a close call. "Roger that. Commencing emergency repair."

A patch on fissures might postpone catastrophic failure… then again it might not. Though she could not see them, someone on the inside of that reflective glass was scrambling to install metal sheet reinforcement even as Brenya reached for the tools at her belt.

The human race had learned long ago that risks

were no longer an option. In order to survive, there had to be layers of safeguards and regulation.

Swaying in her rigging, dangling high above the ground, she tiptoed around the damaged section's frame. With the aid of a heat gun and strong epoxy, Brenya endeavored to reinforce what would ultimately be a fatal crack. It was delicate work that required patience and a light touch. Too much heat, and the whole panel might shatter, too little, and the epoxy would fail to set. One had to account for the sun, the changing outside temperature. One had to adjust to the blinding glare engineering grunts were trained never to turn their head from.

Grunts tasked with the dangerous job of outer Dome repair were *never* to let their eyes wander. The verdant, creeping wilderness could not be a distraction. Staring at the open skyline, the distant tips of a dead, crumbling city's tallest structures were said to encourage mental instability. It endangered all those who relied on them inside to maintain absolute focus.

Those caught looking were grounded and banned from making *the descent* again.

Failure of so grave a nature led to social ostracizing from the very corps one had been raised with, the family one worked with. Colleagues would find you suspicious; friends would demand one submit to reassignment.

Never would Brenya risk it.

Being selected for the external repair program had already placed her in a less than favorable light amongst her peers—even if the work she did kept them all alive.

Every citizen had heard the stories of engineering grunts who grew obsessed with what languished outside the Dome. Some had even tried to leave, or purposefully harmed the structure that protected them all. If rumors were true, there was even a growing faction of dissenters who quietly questioned if the virus was really a threat.

In the five years she'd routinely made the descent, Brenya had seen things outside the Dome people inside would never lay their eyes upon. She was privy to what her colleagues considered temptation. Once a butterfly alit beside a ventilation duct she was reconstructing piece by piece. The insect had been spotted orange and lightly fluttered its wings as it rested so near her fingers could almost brush it. She had wanted to watch that insect, to marvel at nature as her ancestors must have done before the plague. But it was forbidden.

Before the increase in her heart rate might signal to her tech a break in protocol, she'd shooed it away. As far as Brenya knew, no soul in the Dome had ever known that, for a matter of seconds, she understood why some grunts grew obsessed with all that lay outside.

"*Unit 17C, weather forecasting warns an 18 knot gust will arrive from the north in twenty seconds.*"

"Roger."

With skilled movement, she reached for the magnetic handholds stored in the utility belt around her bio-suit. Swinging her rigging to the left, they were locked into place on an undamaged panel. By the time the wind rushed past her, she was secure, pressed to the side of the Dome, and safe.

It was the second, undeclared gust five minutes later that was her ruin.

While dangling upside-down from her harness in an attempt to finalize the last portion of her repair, tearing wind slammed her straight into the pane so hard she lost her breath. It shattered just like Brenya had reported it would, right before she felt a sudden loss of gravity.

Her rigging had failed, the snake-like hiss of rope slipping through her belay loop attachment pulley.

She didn't have time to scream.

Plummeting head first toward the ever encroaching vegetation, the backup catch snapped.

She was going to die.

Twisting in the cables as she fell, a sudden sharp

wrench left her in screaming pain. Jerked to stillness, her arm was caught, her shoulder joint torn from its socket.

Sounds of misery gurgled in her throat, the smallest of breaths almost impossible. The world was upside down. She had fallen so far, hundreds of meters, her dangling arm almost touching the ivy scaling the concrete foundation of Bernard Dome.

Blood rushed to her head, vision going to a pinpoint.

Amidst the crackling call of her tech for a status update, she found herself distracted. She could see them, diminutive simple flowers, her arm reaching towards their vines as if they were a rope and she might pull herself to safety.

She could smell them...

Tears gathered in the corners of her eyes, hot drips running into a damp hairline.

"Unit 17C, your vitals register as erratic and your bio-suit is broadcasting damage to your helmet's visor."

She wanted to answer but couldn't move her lips. She could do nothing but stare at the nine-petaled flowers and try to breathe.

"Report, Brenya!"

Hearing her name, the break in protocol, startled her out of waning consciousness.

One croak, the sound of labored breath, that's all she could offer.

It was as her tech had claimed. More than her body had been damaged; a massive chunk had been knocked from her visor. Brenya had been exposed to open air—could smell the world, the dirt, her sweat. She could even smell her blood where it trickled from a split cheek and into her eye.

"Brenya... you know procedure." There was a hedging desperation the tech tried, and failed, to keep out of his voice. *"Without a status report, you'll be cut from the rigging. I need you to talk to me."*

She had one final thought. *I'll miss you too, George...*

Her stomach roiled and unconsciousness won out.

IT WAS dark by the time her swollen eyelids blinked apart. Body rocking in the breeze like a spider at the bottom of its silk, Brenya hung limp. She couldn't see from her right eye, it was too gooey with blood, but if she squinted, she could just make out shapes in the moonlight.

Warm air brushed her cheek.

For the first time in Brenya's life, she recognized what real weather felt like. It was humid and soft. She could even taste it when she swallowed around a fat tongue.

Teeth chattering despite the heat, she managed one word. "George…"

Nothing.

Sweat saturated her hair, dripping up pounding temples. "Thiiis is… this issss Unit 17C. I require assistance." She tried to move to see if she might turn her body right-side up. "I'm caught in the rigging, and I can't move my left arm."

It was a different voice that cracked through the static. *"Your suit shows an increase in body temperature. Exposure to outside contaminants must be considered."*

The Red Consumption?

No…

She'd slipped midday. That infamous disease killed in a matter of hours. It was night now. If she'd been exposed to Red Consumption, she'd already be dead.

Another, blessedly familiar voice interjected. *"Sir, her temps were up prior to the climb. Unit 17C is documented as running hot."*

Oversight would never believe she was uninfected if her every breath continued to rattle. She had to get herself stable if she wanted to survive.

She had to prove she was viable, that she could still serve.

Shoulder aching, she could feel how swollen it was, but in a very unnerving way, it didn't *hurt*. With a left arm that would be useless and a right arm caught to her chest, only her legs might set her free. Straightening them was harder than expected. First her right leg wrapped around the traitorous cable, left leg pushing off from Bernard Dome's foundation.

She unrolled so fast, Brenya was in a scramble to find a grip before she fell to her death. Bloated fingers caught air, tore at her suit, and finally, *finally*, a glove found the friction of sliding rope. Where the strength came from, she could not tell, but she found herself holding on with one hand so close to the ground, her boots could feel the spongy give of the white flowered ivy's leaves.

The sound of her own heavy breathing echoed through her earpiece, a strained grunt all she could offer the team listening in on the other end. Feet to the wall, Brenya began to climb, one handed, until she found a way to loop her only lifeline back through the harness.

Arm burning, panting in huge gulps of tainted air, she let go. The moment she sat back safely in the rigging, the strangest thought crossed her mind.

It was jasmine... the white flowers were jasmine.

She'd never smelled anything so beautiful.

"I have reattached and will proceed to the nearest decontamination hatch. Please advise."

No response crackled in her ear.

Over the next several hours, no assistance arrived to help Brenya scale the Dome—though she made continuous status reports while creeping up the side like a bug.

Oversight was watching. George was silent.

When she finally crested the nearest hatch, she was left waiting for those inside to decide if she might live or die. Brenya was exhausted, and Oversight's accusation was true: she did not feel well.

Her left arm hung throbbing at her side and required immediate medical attention. She was thirsty, so very thirsty that her tongue stung even worse than the crusted gash on her cheek.

They left Brenya waiting until sunrise. Dozing against the hatch, she felt it give, scuttling to her feet before she might fall. The mechanized door opened, the first of five decontamination chambers waiting.

Had her uniform not been damaged, all she would be required to do was stand on the mark, arms raised and legs spread. Fire would blast the outside of the bio-suit, heating her to the point skin would almost blister underneath. Unfortunately, with her suit damaged and the helmet's visor in shambles, incineration decontamination would equal death.

The room's COM boomed, *"Unit 17C, you are to remove your bio-suit and place it on the mark for incineration."*

Fumbling with the catches and clasps, leaning against the wall because her legs shook, she pulled off the broken helmet and tossed it where it would be burned to ash. Gloves, boots, the suit, every stitch of her protection was peeled from clammy skin, the female hissing when her swollen shoulder refused to budge from within its sleeve.

Tears running down a bloody face, she had to force her arm free, praying to the gods muffled screams would stay locked behind tight lips.

When it was done, she stood in sweat soaked underclothes, and the hatch to the world with white, scented flowers hermetically sealed. In the next few moments, Brenya would discover whether or not this was to be her crematorium.

A click made her jump, set her already racing heart into her throat. The room's only other door, the door that would lead to potential salvation, swung inward.

The chamber beyond was lit, and there were crates stacked right in the center of the space. While she had been waiting outside, a cot had been set up, emergency rations left in a bin.

Dashing forward, she entered decontamination room two.

Once sealed in, she was not allowed to leave the cramped space. Only basics were left to see to her body's needs. When the bio-suit protected scientists charged with observing the specimen came to administer a daily barrage of tests, they took her full bucket and brought a fresh one.

Beyond the point of embarrassment, she let them poke and prod, take samples and scrapings. If they told her to spit, she spit. If she was ordered to take off her clothing, she stripped at once.

She ate from the supply crate's rations and drank stale water from emergency pouches older than she was.

She had always been obedient, just as she had always been a dedicated hard worker. Like the other Betas in her unit, Brenya Perin of Palo Corps, was fiercely loyal to Bernard Dome's combined effort of survival and prosperity.

From the best she could reason without a watch or window, quarantine extended over two weeks—most of that time spent alone with nothing to do, no one to talk to. The only reason she knew freedom had been earned, was a slight shift in routine—the medic who'd set her shoulder the first day, who'd given her a sling to wear over dirty underclothes, had returned.

After a thorough exam, he offered a fresh jumpsuit.

He then instructed Unit 17C to vacate the decontamination chambers and rejoin her people. Pride made her smile under the stitches in her cheek. Pulling her suit zipper up under her chin, eager to go home, she smoothed her tangled bob of lank hair, careful of her damaged arm, and walked, surrounded by bio-suit clad scientists, out to greet waiting friends.

Clearing the final room, she found no joyous party—not even George, the tech Brenya had worked with for five years.

It was not until she returned to her bunk at Palo Corps barracks that word she'd been grounded until further notice arrived. The women she had known since birth, the ones she had been raised with, educated with—the ones she'd played with and thought of as sisters—all one-hundred who shared the room kept their distance.

Brenya had never willingly looked at the horizon. She had not studied the shapes of leaves or how the wind moved the trees. It didn't matter. Unit 17C was counted as one of the tainted.

That first night, she cried in her bunk, wishing

she had never seen the white flowers or smelled jasmine on the wind.

Every morning when the call was made to rise, she would watch her fellow Betas climb from their cots and dress in the uniform of their zone. She too wore the grey jumpsuit, she too broke bread in the mess hall with her sisters, but unlike them, she no longer had an assigned purpose.

Oversight, it seemed, believed Brenya had nothing to offer to the collective.

After a week living as a borderline pariah, after endless skewed looks and terse answers to attempted conversation, she found she could no longer choke down meals. She stopped eating. Her head ached; her stomach was always in knots. To prove herself useful, Brenya had taken to unordered janitorial work. With her good arm, she scrubbed the toilets, the floors, the walls, every surface inside her barracks. When she ran out of things to clean, she walked East Sector looking for debris on the ground.

It was two days of garbage collection before she found herself outside the gates separating the various engineering corps from the techs and central Oversight.

George would help her… it's not like she didn't recognize that he had been the one to save her life. He would help her earn an assignment and end this torment. But Brenya was denied entry. The Alpha guard sneered behind his helmet once she'd been scanned, her rank and designation displayed.

To her shame, she felt her lip shake. "Please."

He looked to her sling, to the gash atop her cheekbone that would scar and remind everyone why her face was marred: an engineering grunt's visor had broken, unit 17C had breathed contaminated air.

She was infected, even if she was not.

When she continued to stand there, waiting as if he might change his mind, the Alpha guard raised a hand to her damaged shoulder. It was not a gesture of comfort or reassurance. Instead, he used his grip to shove her away.

Before those free to come and go, before all who kept their distance, Brenya fell. Crying in earnest, she put her hand to her throbbing shoulder and cowered.

No one made a move to help, though she could see a reflection of pity in the expressions of those nearest. When she could not bear the shame another moment, she tucked her feet under her body. Brenya made herself stand no matter how dizzy she'd become. Stumbling step by step, the woman wandered like a kicked dog in the direction of her barracks.

Halfway through the journey, she was distracted

by the sound of running water. Overhot and fevered, sweat beaded at her temples. Upon seeing the fountain sparkling at the center of East Sector's square, there was a change in course.

Laziness was frowned upon, but Brenya sat there at the water's edge, taking in the beauty of a precious piece of art installed in the Dome before the gates were sealed. This relic had once sat outside the Place de la Concorde. Who designed it, she could not say. Art history was not emphasized amongst those chosen for an engineering education. Just as she could not tell how old it was or why it was culturally important to her people.

What she could say was that dipping her hand into that cool water, wiping her feverish face felt more beautiful than any fountain might ever be. Just as she put her lips to that sparkling blue resting in her palm, a roar cut through the air. Backing away from her perch, her eyes darted around the superstructure for a sign of what ogre might have made so terrible a noise.

She heard the roar again, closer.

There was this violent sense of inevitability, the icy feeling of impending doom. She could not tell you what came over her, why that noise threw her into such a panic, but she could say that never in her life had she run so fast.

Blood was pounding behind her eyes, her legs

wobbling as if under the influence of some unknown drug. She'd almost made it to her barracks—where all she wanted was to climb under the blankets and hide.

Almost…

2

Arms came fast and rough around Brenya. No matter how she tried to dig her heels into the sidewalk, the flailing woman couldn't plant a foot on the ground. She was being dragged, the strength of a massive body hard at her back. She wanted so badly to be free, to call for help past the hand pressed over her mouth, but frantic struggles amounted to nothing.

Hauled off the main causeway down a dead-end ventilation duct, Brenya could hardly breathe, too weak from the innate feebleness brought on by days of fasting. Before she could squirm away, her body was turned, pinioned between an unforgiving wall and the alarming presence of a colossal Alpha.

If unconditional dominance could be focused into

a single creature, if it could be compressed, forced under one's skin into the shape of a man, then Brenya was looking upon it. He had power in just one glance, the kind that exists without reason or fairness.

Over the endless whoosh of the duct's massive fan, she lost her scream.

Their eyes met and the sound was never born from her throat. His were the intensity of hellacious rage, the shade of envy, and deadly focused. He leaned closer as she trembled, his large hand enclosing about the female's throat.

Nostrils flaring, he sucked in an extended breath.

Jade eyes rolled back in his head.

Panting, slapping his body so he might release his mass from smashing her further into the building did nothing more than earn a snarl from the male. He wanted his hostage still and silent.

Skin crawling, feeling as if she were on fire, Brenya dared to claw at the great hand encircling her throat. As if to acquiesce to the frantic plea, his grip abated, fingers trailing to the collar of her grey jumpsuit.

He was going to kill her—she could smell the aggression on the Alpha and began to cry. All she could think of was how she'd brought such an outcome on herself. She should never have tried to get through the gate. She should not have drunk from the fountain.

She was to be arrested and punished.

Frantic to explain, to earn release, Brenya whimpered, "Please. I'm sorry."

As if she had never spoken, the male pinched the tab of her zipper. The grinding release as it descended down her neck confounded the woman. A tan clavicle grew exposed, the rise and fall of her chest all the more obvious. When her sling stopped his progress, before the fabric might part further, the Alpha's knee batted her thighs apart. He'd hoisted her up so his nose might burrow against that freshly bared skin.

At the feel of his tongue rasping over flesh, Brenya's panic hit a fever pitch. She screamed, more frantic writhing drawing a deeply disturbing growl from her attacker. His reverberating threat continued, even as his mouth descended to devour the female's shrieks. It was as if he might swallow her up, his lips sliding, a serpentine tongue dipping in to stir up every syllable, to distort her pleas.

It was the lack of air, of bearing the weight of so much man pressed against her. Her insides began to burn. She could feel them systematically squeezing, cramping, coming apart until she was no longer crying for freedom, but whimpering from pain.

The smell of that stranger was heady, thick and salty… and nothing like jasmine.

Her stomach rebelled; she gagged.

Why an Oversight Alpha was there, why he'd pinned her against that wall and felt free to touch her, she could not say. It was rare for elites of such rank to enter Beta sectors, though it was not the first time Brenya had laid eyes on the ones who governed. But never had she seen this one. Never had she been close enough to one to feel that under their strange Centrist's clothing, they were every bit as strong as their mass broadcasted.

Never had she shared breath with one.

Sweating profusely, she grew slippery in his grip. Or at least that's why she thought her squirming had finally pulled the shackles of his hands away. She was wrong.

Her good arm was not enough to bat the male's touch off when he reared and grabbed the front of her uniform. He didn't even bother with the caught zipper. He wrenched cloth until the covering split down the front and breasts bounced free. And then he was touching them, palming the meaty flesh half hidden by a sling.

Gasping, unable to shove him back, she tried to beg him to stop, but his mouth ate up all noise.

Everywhere his fingers touched, skin burned. He was a brand, Brenya on fire.

There were laws against this sort of thing. There were laws that were supposed to protect females from terrifying Alphas—laws that forbade a male from reaching lower into her torn jumpsuit to poke at the place between her legs.

Blunt fingers ran the length of her slit, a squeal caught in the mouth of the male who would not stop tasting her tongue.

More fabric tore. He growled, and she was going to be sick. Brenya did not see how or even see when he'd reached between their bodies to free his member. She was not sure how he hitched her legs wider, or how he lined up. What she did know was that she buzzed as if being chopped up by that whirring fan when the Alpha drove home.

Once inside, he began to hush her... as if his captive's panic had finally registered. "Shhhhhhh."

"...please."

A groan so filthy she shuddered, came from the beast. He lessened his grip on her knees, gravity pulling Brenya farther down a shaft she was sure would split her in two.

That engorged torture device could not be made to go deeper, the male frustrated that she was too small.

Hips jerking, he began to rut, bouncing her body back against the wall, his every thrust marked with an animalistic grunt.

Brenya gave up. She gave up and cried, eyes roving to find that at the end of the dank alley a few spectators stood by and did nothing while she was publicly mounted.

These things did not happen in Bernard Dome.

Teeth grazed her throat. She heard him whisper, "*Mon petit chou*"—my little sweetheart.

Fluid gummed up sore thighs, made him slip and stretch a part of her that ached and smelled of blood.

The graze of his tongue traced from the hollow of her throat to the tip of her chin, the male pulling back to meet dulled eyes. He brought those swollen lips to the shell of the poor girl's ear. Even as he grumbled, there was no pause in the upward pistoning of his hips. "*Mon chou*, you must relax and accept me or my knot will hurt you."

"Please…"

She could feel the horror of what he referred to, a bulbous thing growing outside her opening. He'd failed to fully penetrate, no matter how he'd thrust. If he thought to shove that inside her, she knew she would die.

One arm hitched under her bottom, the other circling her neck, he bent her back, he opened her up. The sound that came from him as he pressed his cock forward, nothing in the world had ever unnerved her so deeply. Legs shaking, the lower half of her body lost in convulsions, those last inches burrowed their way into her organs. The growing knot was at her lower lips, she could feel its heat and pulse. When he forced it forward, the thing popped past the threshold and he fully invaded her body—only for his cock to expand to a point the pressure on her bladder grew, and she was certain she would urinate.

Something else came out of the female, strange smelling fluid squirted between their bodies, dripped down her rear, onto his legs, and all over the cobblestone ground.

The stranger ground his hips, still rutting as much as their joined bodies would allow. His sack tightened and the man cried out.

Mouth open in a silent scream, she felt it, that first wave of fire. He dumped an ocean of seed inside her, the Alpha coming over and over until Brenya was certain she would burst.

Eyes closed, she felt the nature of his touch alter. Above where his cock destroyed her, his thumb began to play. "That's it, sweet girl."

She knew what it was he touched—the nerve bundle that made mating pleasurable for Beta females. Parting her lashes to look down from where her head hung, she found hers swollen and distended from the abuse.

He was playing with her, sliding his slippery touch in insistent circles. All it led to was cramps and a wave of scorching fire. Brenya felt them consume her, burn through her veins until her insides began to rhythmically squeeze, and he began to groan. On and on it went, her body bowed and legs mindlessly kicking.

She had zero control. She had no way of stopping it. It hurt—the worst pain she'd ever known—but it also felt as if the gods had filled her with sunlight, and it was that light that was going to incinerate her very being. Orgasm they called *la petite mort,* the little death, and in that moment, Brenya finally understood why.

SOUND, the whimpers of a wounded animal, woke her. Every exhale held a whine, every inhale the shallow sounds of fear. Three breaths deep and Brenya realized that pathetic music was coming from her.

Soft linen lay under her cheek, body completely cocooned where she'd curled into a tight ball. Her good hand was pressed between bruised thighs, every muscle on fire, but it was nothing to the burn between her legs.

When she thought she might faint from the heat, a cool cloth passed over her forehead, her cheek, sweet ice trailing down her neck.

Somewhere behind her a man spoke, his voice tired. "Blood tests are conclusive. The Omega has not entered proper Estrous. Due to an inundation of Beta chemical conditioning, her body has turned on itself with misfired signals, fever, and an inflamed nervous system."

"How is it that no one knew what she was?"

That low rumbled timbre she recognized. Knowing it was *he* who lingered so close, who touched her, sent Brenya into a panic. She tried to squirm away but could hardly move before a much stronger body was pressing her back. "Hush now, my girl. You're safe."

Safe? Was he insane?

"No..." Pleas were jumbled, Brenya blubbering as if under an ocean of boiling tar. "Don't."

"Rest." That cool cloth was pressed gently to her marred cheek. "I won't leave you."

A nearby feminine voice suggested, "Maybe you should leave..."

An Alpha's answering growl silenced the unknown female. "You are here to witness, not to speak, Annette."

The female offered a timid, "She's afraid of you, Jacques."

"She's sick." A hand settled on Brenya's skull, fingers threading through tangled hair. "She's confused. That's all. She doesn't understand what was done or why."

The other presence in the room, the one her blurred vision could only just see outlined behind the monster pinning her down, began to read off whatever report was before him. "Brenya Perin was listed as flawed—marked seven years ago as an inferior genetic Beta representation. That is the reason she has never been optioned for the breeding bank. She was never exposed to us, only noted for agreeing to partake in pleasurable coitus a handful of times since she came of age."

The Alpha's voice grew chilling. "Who fucked her?"

"Two Betas are listed here. More than twenty petitioned requests. It seems she only met the expected quota for mental health and nothing more."

Her captor was less concerned with whether or not it was considered mentally hygienic to share pleasure, but instead infuriated over the fact another male had been sanctioned to touch her on more than one occasion. "Who did she allow to rut her repeatedly?"

"A Beta from Tech Sector, George Gerard. Before she was grounded, they shared a working relation-ship. His dossier states the male is serving three months in lockup for interfering with safety protocols after the decision was made to abandon your Omega outside the Dome. From what I see, you have him to thank for her survival—they were going to cut her loose." The sound of paper flipping preceded, "He may even be ultimately responsible for forcing her body off chemical restraint. The Omega's weeks in seclusion, her access to untreated rations, aggravated her endocrine system. Otherwise, Brenya may never have shown Omega characteristics. Her whole life might have been wasted laboring as a Beta."

Wasted? She was one of the best engineering grunts under the glass. She had conducted dangerous maintenance on their Dome that had enriched millions of lives. How dare he!

"She's in pain. Give her more morphine." Cool fingers traveled from the shell of her ear down the length of a soft neck. At the curve before her shoulder, they lightly danced atop the still mottled skin. Though the male's presence made her cringe, something in that soft rapping eased her growing irritation. "What can be done for her fever?"

She heard a sigh that hinged on exasperation, felt the prick of a needle in her arm. Even in her muddled state, she could sense his annoyance was not for the Alpha, it was directed toward her. Brenya was the root of his problem. "Nothing. She has not responded to conventional treatment. As her illness is tied to this retarded estrous, her fever may not go down for days, maybe a week... maybe longer. Omega physiology is not designed to withstand a lifetime of Beta pharmacology. Polluted as she is, her system is stuck and at war with itself. I cannot even assure you she will survive. This woman should never have been put in Palo Sector to be exposed to their food and water supply."

The Alpha spoke with such carelessness, "If she dies, you die next."

No! Brenya's purpose was to protect life, her oaths sworn every morning since she was old enough to stand. Breath coming in short pants, she tried to focus. Her good hand reached out, gathering the Alpha's sleeve in her fist. "Don't hurt him."

A low chuckle came from the male stroking her cheek. Running his fingertips over her lips, he said, "Look at me, *mon chou*."

She tried. After blinking repeatedly, she centered upon her personal hell. *Him.* It was hard to focus, but she saw the tawny gold of his hair, she saw eyes brighter than the water at the fountain.

"Good girl." Lips that were defined and full pressed against hers. "You want to help him? Then you must recover. Once you do, I'll be yours to command."

At her groaned complaint, noise reverberated more loudly from his chest. Only then did she

realize the Alpha was purring—had been purring all
along.

Brenya had heard of this thing. Once or twice
she'd even experienced a muted copy, but to *feel* an
Alpha purr was unlike anything she'd known. It
wasn't just the sound. That noise moved through a
body, it shook tired places… it settled. Even terrified as she was, she melted.

Or had, until a cramp made the tender flesh
between her legs sear. Gasping, she reached down
and felt a fresh flow of liquid rush from her body.

The Alpha's overbearing musk began to stink
like it had in the alley. She did not need to open her
eyes to know he'd licked his lips.

"She's wetting through the sheet again. It might
not be continuous, but her slick grows more abundant. My Omega will endure. Soon, I will be able to
claim her."

"Not soon. You tore her, Jacques. The vaginal
fissures…" The older male approached. To Brenya's
horror, he flipped up the sheet covering her lower
half. But before he might touch her, a feral growl
rent the air. The sound of a weighty bulk slammed
against the wall, it shook the room, and the old
man's groans led her to lean up.

As she was pushed back down, Brenya saw a
small woman heavy with child trying to help a grey-
haired old man to stand. Awkward as she was with

so large a belly, she didn't stop until her shoulder was under his, until she faced her host and my captor.

"Jacques, enough."

"Go to your husband, Annette. Tell him what you saw here, and know he will laud me for not killing the fool who thought to expose my estrous high mate."

Brenya could not see clearly enough to see if the woman scorned such a statement. But she heard no complaint, only the sound of a door unlatching before two ponderous bodies squeezed through.

Then they were alone.

The injection, the morphine, was doing its work. She was muted, caught in a place where the cease-less purr was so distracting she wanted to swim through it. Even the pain began to dissipate.

His face, she could not stop looking at his face. Alphas were visually appealing. They looked *different* than Betas, more refined... bigger. Still, she would have rather had any other man in the world smiling down at her.

"None of this is your fault, Brenya." His hand edged nearer where the sheet was sticky with what had gushed from her body. "You've been the ideal citizen. As Commodore, I commend you. Now, *mon chou*, you have a new task. You are to get better, the rest we can discuss afterward."

She felt a squiggle between her legs. A slender warmth breached her, pumped cautiously through the river flowing from her private place.

As he fingered her, he spoke. "I owe you an ocean of apologies for what transpired when we met. You are the first Omega born under Bernard Dome in three generations. I may have been overzealous in securing you once I caught your scent."

There was a sting, a stretch between her legs, the Alpha adding another finger to prod and twist inside.

"What are you doing?"

The beast had the audacity to smile. "Only I can offer what your body needs, sweet girl. You're in a form of estrous. Without stimulation you will suffer."

Before she might try to squirm away, she was flipped carefully onto her belly, his weight settling on her back. Strong arm tucked under her hip, those same fingers went right back into their slippery home, even with her legs pressed tightly shut. On and on it went until Brenya was certain she was going mad.

Pump, squirm, twist, part—over and over, until she hissed that what he was doing was not enough. She had not meant to, could not tell you what had possessed her to moan as she did. At her loudest drugged complaint, she was pressed again to her back, the massive man lowering between spread thighs. His fingers continued to gently spear her, but it was his mouth that made her scream.

There was no shame as he smiled and flicked his tongue over swollen lower lips. He tormented her clitoris, sucking, rolling, and dragging it about while his hand twisted until she thought she might go mad.

The fever, the pain, was forgotten. Brenya saw white, pure light—remembered the warmth of the breeze outside the Dome. For a moment, she was certain she could smell jasmine.

At the moment *the little death* came upon her, his teeth skimmed her inner thigh. He bit down. When the skin broke, it was the most exquisite pain.

3

"More…"

Warm air moved over Brenya's ear, the weight of thick limbs circling like a python squeezing its prey. "What do you need, dearest?"

She was not fully awake, and it took her a moment to recognize that she had been the first to speak. Blinking, she took in the room. Around where she was kept, curtains had been drawn, enclosing herself and her captor in shadows. Linen under her nose was wrinkled and heady with male scent and the acrid stink of her perspiration.

Everything was muddled, all Brenya held were fragments of memory, but sometimes she knew to be afraid. She was lying in *his* bed—these were *his* rooms where she had been forced to convalesce.

In her stupor over the last few days, more than once she'd tried to leave, stumbling drunkenly from bed as if she might find a door in the dark. Each time, muscled arms had swept her up, returning her to the cocoon of soft blankets and strong limbs.

The other half of the time her mind was so fogged she forgot to be afraid, forgot where she was. Everything converged into simple sensation. Sometimes the male exercised the power to make her feel very good. Other times, just his presence, the lightest brush of his touch was agony.

The air was so saturated, she could taste him in every breath, was so soaked in his sweat, she felt as if that aroma must have seasoned her down to her bones.

"Shhhhh, Brenya." Sensation trickled down her spine, the Alpha crouching over her, running his tongue down each vertebrae. He kneaded the space between her shoulder blades, tugged gently at the roots of her hair. "Be still and peaceful."

Teeth came to her earlobe, his great weight settling over her back. Something about the way he crushed her against the bed, every time he had done it, quieted fear. He took control. She emptied her mind because she had no other choice. Tranquility was enforced.

These short lapses of peace never lasted. Something would invade reason... his smell, the weight of his body. Brenya would find her head turned, her cheek to his neck. Sometimes in the fever, she relished the burn his skin inflicted on hers. Once she'd even found herself licking that muscled column much to his delight.

And then excruciating pain came.

It tore at her insides until she screamed.

Gods how she hated it, what he'd do to her when agony twisted her limbs. His weight would abate. She would be uncurled no matter how she fought him, and forced to lay upon her back. Each of her wrists would be shackled in a grip of iron, arms spread open while she raged.

His answer to her suffering was to watch her and make her watch him.

He would talk. More often than not, Brenya did not understand a word.

"It's time to listen to me, *mon chou*." When he spoke so coolly and she felt so horrid, she longed to claw out his eyes.

"Brenya, I'll tie you to the bed if I must."

She fought to be free, biting.

The Alpha barked, "Cease this unit 17C!"

Instantly, still as a corpse she lay, eyes staring straight ahead, anticipating orders.

"Open your legs for me."

She didn't, but relaxed the stranglehold keeping them together.

"Unit 17C, have I harmed you once since you woke in this bed?"

Staring at the ceiling, eyes unfocused, she said, "I am an engineering grunt. My assignment is outer Dome maintenance. I am late to my post."

Sterner, he gave her a little shake. "Have I given you pain?"

There was a wave of unfamiliar feeling. All at once Brenya felt very sad, completely alone, and she really needed to pee. She looked at the Alpha tormenting her and whined, "My arm hurts."

A smile split that sculpted face. The tip of his tongue licked up her tears. "Poor darling, the dislocated joint will be uncomfortable for some time. But, did I cause that pain?"

"No." He had caused the pain everywhere else. "I fell down the side of the Dome."

Her wrists were joined above her head so he might hold them with just one hand. The tips of his free fingers moved from her brow, down the edge of her face, to hook and stroke from jaw to chin. "You woke asking for something. Tell me, *mon chou*, what you desire?"

It was the feeling, the weight of that part of him that was always engorged, always erect. The heftiness of his cock draped over her belly, the slide of him a little slippery from sweat and the tiny, scented drips that continued to fall from his fat crown, they were magnetic.

Her eyes automatically went to that swollen member. More fluid pulsed from its tip, pooling at her navel.

The man groaned when he followed her line of sight. Reaching between them, his finger collected the sticky glob. Her jaw was pinched until teeth parted, and between her lips that mess was smeared.

This was not the first time.

The very thought of what he was doing disgusted her, the way he forced it in, the way he made sure it was spread all over her tongue. But the taste, oh my gods, the taste had a power of its own. She sucked it from his fingers like a starving woman might lap honey straight from a buzzing hive.

Another of those cramps came, ushering after it a wave of warm fluid. Brenya released every last drop of what she had been struggling to retain. Slippery, the puddle grew, and her cramping stopped. Eyes burning in shame to have made another mess, she could never understand why the Alpha smiled each time she'd ruined the bed.

As if he could read her thoughts, he pulled his fingers from her lips and looked at what saturated the linen. His hand slipped over soggy sheets, cupping what he could catch, moving to her belly to rub it into soft skin. "This is beautiful to me,

Brenya. Omegas are supposed to secrete *slick* for their Alphas. You honor me. There is no need to try and hold it in."

Fully ashamed, she found her tongue. "What is slick?"

"Omegas create abundant lubrication to ease the entrance of an Alpha's cock. You produce it now because you are sexually aroused."

Sex...

She could feel the burn between her legs as if reliving the nightmare when he'd shoved that part of his body into hers. "Don't do it again. Don't, please. Oh Gods, pleeeease!" She could not stop herself, was practically groveling at the memory of the wall at her back, the terror. "I am sorry I looked at the flowers. I didn't mean to break my helmet. I never observed the butterfly, it just landed there."

"Hush, hush, hush..." His hand slithered between their bodies until the part of her that trembled and wept was touched. Cautiously, he pushed two digits inside. "We will suffer through this tainted estrous together, and until you have healed and are properly prepared, I swear I will not fuck you again. You have my word. What happened in Beta Sector, my loss of control, I will atone for it. I will deny myself release no matter the rut. Do not be afraid."

Muscles clenched around his fingers, her mouth

letting loose a low moan when he twisted deeper. "Why is no one stopping this?"

"Breathe, Brenya." His tongue swept her mouth, slithered down her throat, between her breasts, all the way down to where he pressed her thighs apart. "You are safe, and I will never hurt you."

And then it began all over again.

She squealed as his fingers toyed with the nerves inside her body, sobbed at the rough feel of his tongue moving through tender folds. The following screams were not inspired by pain.

No, those shrieks belonged to hysteria and the strange sense that she was going insane.

"You seem very satisfied with yourself, Jacques." A man, another large Alpha bearing an impossibly deep voice, spoke from across the parlor.

The male stood far from where Brenya sat, his bulk leaning against the door. His hair was long, dark, and bound back into a queue—worn in the same fashion as all other Alpha males. One look at him had made her frown.

She recalled his cat-like features from the alley when Jacques had...

The dark-haired one had stood at a distance then too, watching while his host had fucked her senseless. He had watched, and he had done nothing. "I remember you."

Head dipping once, the terms of their first meeting were acknowledged. "You look well."

An upwelling of spite distorted her voice. "You didn't help me. An Alpha's duty is to protect Betas. That is your purpose in our population."

The stranger across the room spoke calmly. "When you come to understand the importance of that moment, you will forgive me."

Her brows fell. This new room, this parlor, was as bad as the bedroom. Her former barracks were infinitely superior. They were organized, for one. Everything had its place. Here there was just glittering stuff that served no purpose.

There was a cup of tea in her hand. Her nakedness was covered in soft clothing. No longer was she dirty, burrowed in sticky sheets, the weight of Jacques' body holding her down in the dark. This room was bright, the surroundings rich, sunlight abundant. Under her feet was a rug so sumptuous, pressing bare toes to it felt unnatural. The chair she had been placed in was covered in silk damask, the texture of it slippery and cool. Brenya had never seen items like this in Beta Sector. Everything from the papered walls to the opulent ornamentation was alien.

She longed for the familiar grey of her jumpsuit.

Uniforms made all equal. This strange, diverse clothing these peculiar people wore did not make sense.

At her side, that familiar vibration began, *his* purr growing louder until she took a deep breath and sank back into the chair.

Going back to his Alpha guest's original question, Jacques, my captor, smiled, drinking me in. "And why should I not be pleased, Ancil? My mate is perfect."

Mate...

That word was foreign to Brenya.

"*Mon chou*, say hello to my friends, Ancil, Bernard Dome's Security Advisor, and his wife, Annette."

Only very close intimates used given names. Even Jacques had never told her his name. She'd only heard others speak it. Names were personal; these people were strangers. Her lips parted, protocol all Brenya had to rely on in this new, unsettling place. "I am Unit 17C of Palo Corps."

The third, and least menacing guest, pouted. The petite blonde Beta woman Brenya vaguely remembered standing over her that first day had a sweet look to her, a delicacy brought out by her floral dress and round belly. "But your name, dear, is Brenya. What we were before is left behind when we are called by an Alpha."

The Beta female's explanation did not seem to please Jacques. His voice quiet, his intentions loud, he spoke, "Centrists do not use designations. You have been reassigned here, and will follow your Commodore's directives. Now, introduce yourself properly to our guests."

Annette's kind suggestion, her reasons, had not shifted Brenya's feelings on the topic. But as if Jacques understood how she was wired, how much she clung to procedure, his orders focused her thoughts. Face blank, voice robotic, she obeyed. "My name is Brenya Perin."

Purring loudly, stern, he leaned closer. "And what are you?"

"An engineering grunt responsible for the exterior maintenance of Bernard Dome."

"No." Hardening his expression, the man lowered his chin and very slowly shook his shining head in the negative. Eating up every last ounce of her awareness, he growled, "You are an Omega, *mon chou*."

She felt as if he'd put the words on her tongue. They were not hers, they tasted foreign, and she did not want to swallow them down. "I am an Omega."

"Good girl."

Those watching may have found such an offering sweet, but Brenya saw the predator in those

glinting teeth. Right there in the gleam of Jacques'
eyes laid a promise her soul was his.

No one in this room questioned what he'd done,
or how she'd come to be there. Not one of them
seemed to care that she wanted out.

Jacques possessed more than total control.

When her eyes floated to Annette, the pregnant
woman favored her with a kind smile and wink.
"I've known Jacques since I was a little girl, and
have never seen him dote on anyone... or heard him
speak so gently." Giggling, utterly impish, she
added, "With the Commodore under your thumb,
you could rule the world."

Brenya didn't know what the designation
Commodore meant. She didn't understand anything
here.

"Annette." The hissed reprimand had come from
the dark-haired Alpha at her back. Ancil was not at
all pleased with his wife. "Your wit is not appreciated. You will watch your tongue before the
Commodore."

Waving a hand and glancing over her shoulder
to her husband, Annette disagreed. "He doesn't
mind. His mate is bored, that's why we're here. You
men can blather to one another with politic speech
in parliament. We're at tea, and I would like to see
Brenya smile."

The man dressed like an ancient king, the one

lounging as if he owned the world, found the couple's exchange amusing. "Speak freely, Annette."

Brenya ventured a question. "What is a Commodore?"

As if at a loss for words, Annette cocked her head, her blonde ringlets bouncing. The question seemed unfathomable to the wide-eyed lady. "My darling…"

Ancil spoke in Annette's place. "The Commodore of Bernard Dome holds highest authority. He is your leader, your chief, your priest. Your mate, Jacques, was anointed with that title, just as his father before him held it, on and on down the Bernard bloodline since the Dome rescued our ancestors."

Her priest? The gentle Beta god had no priests. All were a part of him, making all holy… except Brenya wasn't Beta anymore. That made her godless and alone. Disconnected, she felt desolate. "My orders were always issued from Oversight. Oversight manages the Dome."

Ancil nodded. "Oversight is controlled by Parliament. Parliament is ruled by our Commodore. In essence, your orders have always come from your mate."

Brenya's eyes dragged over the carpet to land on the shined shoes of the man they claimed ruled them all. No wonder no soul had tried to stop him when he'd stolen her from Beta Sector. Jacques owned her —though *mate* seemed the more elegant term.

The weight of this understanding shrank her shoulders. "Wives consent."

"Yes," Annette agreed. "There are petitions, negotiations, ceremonies, everything documented because Alphas and Betas cannot pair-bond. Legal protection for the weaker party must be considered. I envy you. Once you enjoy a true estrous, you and Jacques will become as one harmonious being."

Jacques had repeatedly alluded to this *thing*, this great magic that was going to heal every wound he had inflicted. Brenya had a head for mathematics, for science, and had never been interested in religious babble or romantic fairy tales. The balm of a pair-bond seemed unlikely.

She looked at Jacques' guests, Annette and the dark Ancil. The pair wore rings, he had sired her child, and their contract was public... so lineage could be traced if questioned. These things mattered to Centrists.

Betas rarely ventured into such a union. There was no need to. Children could be produced if one wished, partners could be chosen, and when the baby was weaned and given to Oversight to be educated, the cycle could start again. Offspring grew up well, tests conducted so the child could be placed to assure their happiness and society's enrichment. The women from Brenya's barracks were more family to her than the smiling male who spoke with gentle care and exuded total control.

She was uncomfortable with this concept of mate.

She was uncomfortable being stared at by these three strangers. "Why are all the Omegas gone? Why was I never taught about them?"

Annette's eyes betrayed a tiny sliver of shame. "I could not say."

Brenya's face must have grown stormy, for Jacques briskly interrupted her mental analysis. "Share your thoughts, Brenya."

"You must assume the potential that there are other Omegas living happily in Beta Sector. Probability would be on your side, but Oversight Alphas should leave them alone." It bubbled from her stomach, a wave of strong negative emotion. Her eyes flashed. Lips tight, she met his stare as if for once she didn't fear him. "I was happy, but... you are Commodore... all orders come from you."

He could hear the blame in her voice, and offered a soft look. "Do you think I should be the only Alpha enriched by an Omega? Do you believe those other women should be denied what they truly are?"

Whatever had possessed Brenya dried up. Her

anger waned. Again her voice was colorless. "I hope you don't find any."

"Drink your tea, *mon chou*. You are shivering."

It was an order. Following orders felt natural. The cup went to her lips. She swallowed every scalding drop.

Annette radiated concern, looking at Brenya as if she were some strange thing. "How long is she going to be like this?"

Rolling indolently to brace against the armrest of his chair, Jacques grew beautiful and dangerous. "Sparks of temper are a good sign my Brenya is progressing. Soon enough personality will develop, and you will see the smile you were eager to encourage, Annette. It cannot be easy to relearn what one is."

They began to discuss the Omega as if she were not there. "She is close to crying."

"You misread the signs." Jacques sounded genuinely forlorn. "Brenya is hungry, but cannot eat. She is thirsty, but cannot drink. Her metamorphosis has been uncomfortable."

Brenya looked to the pregnant Beta woman, saw her offered smile, and muttered a hoarse, "I want to go home."

For just a moment Annette's smile wavered, then it grew stronger, her voice purposeful, "My darling, you *are* home. This is your home." Her energetic eyes darted over the room, finding great beauty in every carefully selected item. "And what a grand home it is."

"I want to return to Palo Corps... to my sisters."

Jacques answered for her. "No. They are Beta, you are Omega. The error in your placement has been corrected."

She was never going to be returned to her cot at the barracks—there was no place for her there, her skills were no longer needed—this he had told her every time she'd questioned.

"I know you don't feel well right now, Brenya, but you need to eat something." Annette braced her hands against her chair's frame, struggling to raise her bulk from the seat. The man at her back, Brenya could see by the way her husband tensed that he wished to help her, but he would not dare step deeper into the room.

Ancil was being tolerated only so long as he remained by the door. Not that it stopped him from watching the Omega, or raising his nose to scent the air every so often.

Padding across that opulent carpet, Annette took a seat on the divan at Brenya's side. Kindly, she offered her a plate of sweets, well-meaning in her caution. "You must shore up your strength to assure a speedy recovery."

Jacques had claimed he would not force his cock

back into her body until she was healed. That knowledge was the reason her stomach refused food. But she could not tell Annette such a thing.

Sex was not discussed openly in the Beta Sectors. Such lewd behavior was not encouraged. The girls Brenya knew did not talk of mates and pair-bonds. Those raised and educated together had been warned of imprudent breeding. She'd been an exemplary student. The few times she had consented to fornication, measures had been taken to prevent conception.

Brenya had no attraction for sex, found little interest in the actual act, and only performed the minimum she was expected to. All her interest laid in the pride of labor. Her life had been uncomplicated and even fulfilling.

She had been perfectly content.

Now, she missed the regimented structure of her days, did not understand these Centrists, or why life was so foreign here when all lived under the same Dome. Even their accent, it wasn't hers.

Her speech was vulgar, unmusical in comparison. Amongst these people, it made her selfconscious to see how they cringed at the way she pronounced words.

They didn't dress the same as she did, but were colorful, each person's attire different. In Beta Sector there was specific pride in sameness; there was equality. Centrists, Brenya was learning, found such an idea laughable. And as their voices were honeyed, their food was rich. Every item on the plate Annette offered exuded aromas she'd never known. It looked like it all tasted awful.

Annette patted her hand again. "Eat, before silly Jacques orders you to do it."

The pastry in hand, Brenya stared down at a piece of art. An actual plate made of bone china like the ones on display in the Dome's Museum. Its scalloped, golden edges and hand painted symmetry had come from another era. That plate had belonged to someone before the virus cleansed the world and was a treasure of such value, resting it on her lap made her nervous.

What if she dropped it?

"You look pale."

That impending voice, it made her jump. She had not heard him come closer. She'd been too distracted to see. Head flying up, their eyes met. Her lower lip trembled to find Jacques kneeling at her feet. His hand engulfed her shaking knee.

Brenya wanted to scoot back, to put distance between herself and the massive Alpha, but couldn't. Just like the first time, she couldn't move when under the power of his gaze.

Caught by the frankness of his expression, perplexed and hypnotized, she sat voiceless.

Jacques could tell the effect his nearness inspired, she knew he could.

Brenya was a mouse and he was the hawk, ready to tear her limb from limb.

He leaned closer, her terrorizer, and before she might claw and fight her way free, richness moved from him into her. That low rumble, the perfect steady vibration, came from his mass to saturate her every nerve. The Alpha's purr switched her off, altered her physically, until her breath slowed and her shoulders sank from her ears.

His inquiries never struck her as meek. Each question demanded to be answered. "What has upset you?"

Dry lips parted and Brenya, as always, spoke the truth. "I'm afraid I'll break the plate."

The mournful reply amused the looming male. His eyes softened, his mouth curving up at one corner. "There are hundreds more. It is no matter."

Brow drawing tight, she shook her head. Hundreds? She'd only ever seen twenty or so in the museum. Why would there be hundreds... so many that treasures could be treated as disposable?

Long fingers slipped up to gently pull the dish from Brenya's grasp, drawing her attention back down to the beautiful china. Jacques' purr grew deeper, the man raising a corner of pastry as if to feed her.

They had an audience, the guests taken with the scene that made the Omega acutely uncomfortable.

Annette relaxed, her hand resting on her pregnant belly, her smile wistful.

"Open your mouth, Brenya." Jacques, jade eyes alight, waited for *his mate* to part her lips. "You must eat."

She obeyed, and something sweet hit her tongue. She chewed as she was expected to. She swallowed. Suddenly, she didn't want to see Annette's soft golden curls, she didn't want to feel the intensity of the Alpha by the door, and she did not want to suffer the weight of Jacques' stare.

Skin prickling, Brenya tried again to make things right, to explain why she should not be there. "Please... I didn't mean to drink from the fountain. I was just so thirsty. Let me go home."

"*Mon chou*,"—Jacques wove an arm around her back while tapping another morsel against her lips —"this discomfort and confusion will pass. Once we are fully bonded, you will wonder why you were ever afraid."

Seeking solace, her fingers sought the scar on her cheek, a reminder that she had fallen and smelled jasmine, that she'd served a greater purpose. "There are no other grunts who can deconstruct and repair ventilation as quickly as I can. I have a duty... a purpose. I must serve the Dome."

He took her fingers from her face, brushing a kiss over the scar. "I am Commodore. By serving me, you serve the Dome."

"It shouldn't be this way, Jacques." Annette looked at her childhood friend as if he'd done something very wrong. "Females should be happy to have been found by their mates—but she is terrified. If you bonded to her in this state, you would be forcing her—breaking our most sacred tenets."

Before the absolute look of fury on Jacques face might translate into a scathing reply, Brenya sensed it. Ancil, the massive Alpha across the room, was afraid.

"Annette is passionate and often forgets to think before she speaks." Ancil's hand was out, fingers crooked to call his pregnant wife nearer his body. "I will handle her punishment for this infraction personally."

So much anger twisted under the skin of the Commodore. He hunched as if the Omega had been threatened, his shoulders physically blocking her view of all others in the room.

For whatever reason, Annette was in grave trouble for what she had said.

Brenya could not allow that.

"Jacques." It was the first she'd spoken his name.

Head swung around, his fury no longer rolling

over his guests. Blazing eyes locked on Brenya's, he cocked a brow, silently demanding she continue.

She thought of the only thing she might say to redirect his thinking. "You are Commodore, leader of Bernard Dome. All commands come from you. I have been reassigned to Central Sector to serve as Omega. I have been ordered to recover my health. I will eat as required, but I do not care for sweets."

The way his expression softened through her ramblings, the way he cupped his hands to the side of her face, Brenya felt he was very much appeased.

"The workings of your mind intrigue me. As Commodore, I order you to tell me freely what you like and don't like."

"I like Beta Sector rations."

Smirking, Jacques took her lips in a soft peck. "They are not healthy for an Omega. Sorry, *mon chou*, but you cannot have them."

She had been taught that their food was carefully chosen for maximum nutritional value. "Why?"

Another kiss, this time at the tip of her nose. "We'll discuss that later. For now, I will think of something you might like to eat. Do you trust me?"

She needed his attention to stay on her, not on how Annette cautiously crept nearer her husband. "I did not like the broth you brought me, and I have not liked a single thing on this plate. So, no, I don't think you are suited to choose food I will enjoy. Everything here tastes terrible."

The man chuckled, his eyes, those bizarre, verdant eyes danced. "I had a feeling you would be funny. Would you like to make a bet?"

"Betting is illegal, condemned by Oversight with penalties ranging from fines to imprisonment."

He outright laughed, taken completely with her nonsense and blunt rejoinders. "Then we shall call it a game. The winner gets a prize."

Brenya nodded, her cheeks slightly compressed by his hands. "Okay."

"It has been over a week since you arrived, and your doctor ordered that I can no longer feed you what your body truly craves." His fingertips swiped over her lips, alluding to the fluids he'd fed the Omega in bed—of how she had loved the taste. "My body's offering would only encourage your system to cling to the last traces of estrous, and I hate to see you suffer. But, I will find something for you to enjoy."

She felt her cheeks go red, and it took a great deal of willpower to not glance at Annette and Ancil to see if they understood what he'd said.

Fingers carded through her hair, around her ears, under her chin. "You don't need to be embarrassed. What I shared with you was a healthy offering from an Alpha for his mate. You have been designed to need and enjoy it."

This was not comfortable conversation for Brenya. "What is the game?"

There was something deep inside him, some drive to dominate always. Jacques growled in a way that made her stomach feel funny. "This is the game. I'm playing with you right now, and I am winning."

She was out of her depth.

A small contemplative noise came from her throat, Brenya pouting as she considered. "I am taking Annette's punishment?"

A large portion of Jacques' delight vanished. His voice was much louder, so all might hear. "Only Annette can take her punishment."

This was Brenya's chance. She put her fingers on the Alpha's face in mirror of his touch on her. Shock came to his features, as did distrust. "If the game is to say things that make the other person uncomfortable, I can play." She pat his cheek, just as he had done to her, and whispered, "You dragged me down a ventilation duct, slammed me against a wall, put your hands around my throat. You... hurt me. Ancil watched. Annette saw the aftermath when I was brought here—you'd summoned her to witness. It has upset her because she is capable of compassion. You swore to me you would make amends. Punishing her for desiring to defend a single, confused Omega is in contradiction to your oath."

"You"—Jacques' hands delved into blonde hair. He took her nape, leaning over his prize so it was clear who was in charge—"own me."

Clarity, Brenya had not felt mentally sharp since she'd fallen from the Dome, but in that moment she had it. The tension where he subtly pulled her hair, the scent of him… for just one instant, she liked it.

He had seen the change in her, for again, his eyes began to burn. "*Mon chou*, do you forgive me?"

Sobering from the lapse, Brenya asked. "Did I win the game?"

His mouth ever so slowly descended to hers, the way his lips played languorous. When it was done, when she'd held still without cringing, he sighed. "I'll always let you win."

4

The rising sun cast a brief arcing rainbow through the convex side of the Dome. Perched upon the Commodore's private terrace, wrapped in his robe, Brenya sat in the chair he'd carried her to, she drank the tea he'd poured for her, and knew his eyes never left her face.

She felt utterly alone.

Though his shirtless appearance was beautiful, it was hard to look at him.

He had done something unspeakable to her…

Remnants of his games were all over her body, whether or not his robe might cover them.

It was a beautiful morning, the weather outside the Dome full of silvery skies and the soft threat of a coming light rain in the distance. Nature would wash the dust from the side of Bernard Dome, make it new and shining—a beacon of civilization beside the rot of an ancient lost city.

Rain never fell inside the Dome. Rain would never fall on Brenya's bruised skin, or wash away the dried semen Jacques had drenched her with while it was still dark.

Something unspeakable.

The Alpha seated at her side ran the backs of his fingers down her cheek until he could gently catch her chin and turn her head. "*Mon chou*, why are you crying?"

It was unnatural, her responses. She could not control even a simple physical reaction, had lost all composure to the whims of a body she no longer owned—because it was owned by Jacques Bernard. Brenya was fading away, so whatever it was he longed to encourage in her, the *Omega* taking over her mind, might thrive.

Having already begged for her freedom, having told him point blank that she wanted to be returned to Beta sector, having heard his denials, she was slipping away.

Especially now that he was changing her into *something else.*

He might have turned her head, but her eyes did not follow. Still she looked to the light playing off the Dome as if to ignore him.

"Are you going to answer me?" The firmness of

his voice folded into softness, displaying all the strength she lacked.

Another trail of silent tears fell.

His hand left her chin, fingers lightly wrapping her neck as if he toyed with the idea of pulling her closer—of making her answer. "You enjoyed it last night. Need I remind you of that?"

The Alpha was equal parts threatening and sweet, careful in how he touched her, yet lingering over her throat as if to remind the Omega she stood no chance.

Her eyes. Brown eyes the color of honey... she knew this because he said it often, because he complimented them... shifted in their sockets. A light shadow of dark blond stubble shaded Jacques' cheeks. His eyes were aglow, his features rested. He was not suffering as she was.

He was content. Satisfied.

Even her voice sounded different, carried inflection and pain when before it had been perfunctory. "It wasn't me. You've put a stranger inside my head."

"You don't need to be afraid of emotion." All buried aggression faded from the male. He became infinitely soft, his eyes full of love, his voice careful. "What you are feeling now, is who you always were. You just didn't know yourself."

"I knew myself. I knew my work. I knew purpose."

Settling back in his chair, Jacques took her limp hand and intertwined their fingers. "Near the end of the Reformation Wars over forty Domes were in development. Many failed to seal their doors before plague ruined all their efforts and entire populations were decimated. Half the original Domes never made it past the first year, leaving twenty-two spread over the globe."

It had always been considered uncouth to speak of other Domes outside of lecture, the idea discouraged from a very young age. The fact that Jacques spoke so pointedly of it now, considering context, snagged Brenya's attention... as well as her distaste. "We should not speak of these things."

He ignored her trained response, squeezed her hand, and spoke on. "Approximately two-hundred years have passed since those still fighting in the wars died of plague. Civilization has somewhat stabilized... to a point. But, it is not common knowledge that of the original Domes, only twelve stand now."

Shaking her head, she clarified, "There are twenty-two Domes."

"There are twelve left standing today, Brenya."

He was wrong. She'd been taught about the

other Domes in school. "I can list off their names for you, their locations, their cultures and languages."

"Usually our leadership learns of the reasons a Dome failed: technical difficulties, over-population, disease... war. Sometimes we are left with only questions. But seventeen domes over the last two-hundred years were lost—more than half. The people inside them are dead. So, you must understand that it is imperative order be maintained inside Bernard Dome. Order is what keeps us all alive."

Brenya asked, "Why would we be taught that things are different than they are?"

"Because confidence in the world, a firm knowledge that our species has found its place, lessens fear. Very few people know the truth. For, if I was to tell you that less than a year ago one of the most successful Domes, the Dome most protected from plague, from outside influence, from even my satellites' reach, fell in a bloody civil war, how would you feel?"

The human race had moved past petty squabbles. The human race had advanced itself. War no longer had a place in the world. All these thing Brenya told herself, but fear slipped into her reply. "I would not believe you."

"Thólos Dome was ripped apart from the inside. It is fact."

A cold wash of uncertainty set her skin to gooseflesh, made her breath shallow, and turned down the corners of her mouth. "I don't understand."

"Civil war, Brenya. It could happen anywhere, at any time under the right sort of pressure. In Bernard Dome, our founder, my forefather, set into motion a society structure that made it *improbable* but not impossible. It is my duty, the duty of every Dome leader, to assure their people do not fall into the same trap. Over the generations, we have fine-tuned this plan, amplified it, adjusted as we could. There was some sacrifice... such as the decrease and eventual cessation of Omega births."

He was talking about her, all of it, his entire point was her. "Our founder, Henry Bernard, was a brilliant scientist, exceedingly wealthy, and pragmatic. The initial population did not know what he'd added to the water and the food supply. They did not know they had been emotionally suppressed, that their children and their children's children would be farmed into placement and training to benefit the whole. Like all Betas outside of central, you too were subjected to these restraints—from birth, in fact. Pharmacological control has been added to your food, your water. You have been monitored and conditioned from birth to be complacent, obedient, hardworking, and dedicated. Those Betas who fail parameter tests are removed permanently from society. There is no reassignment. Had you not been Omega, you would have been terminated at your next review."

Brenya knew of at least five citizens who had been reassigned. Three of them had been engineering grunts like her. "Berthe, Amie, Walter..."

"It was done quickly. There was no pain." No remorse waited in Jacques' eyes, and he held tight to her fingers when Brenya tried to pull her hand from his touch. "Termination is done in such a way that they never had a moment of fear. They never knew."

Heart racing, trying to back away but unable to break his hold, she whispered, "You are going to have me killed if I don't let you put that machine inside me again?"

"I am not telling you these secrets to frighten you. I am telling you so you might understand the changes in your body. You are unaccustomed to strong emotion or desire. Last night overwhelmed you. But all these feelings, they are yours, they have just been dampened until now."

There had been times in her life the Brenya had felt adrenaline and fear, her fall from the Dome, for example. But she was more scared in this moment than she knew how to process. "You make it sound as if Betas are slaves."

He dared to reach out with his free hand to toy with the choppy ends of her hair. "Some would argue that they are. Others would say they are honed, happy, and useful. Alphas are also controlled to keep aggression minimal. Only key Centrist families and government officials are excluded."

"Those who were reassigned, all they did was look at the skyline." Panic stole her breath, made her shake. "I've seen it too, you know. You can't go out there and not see it."

"My darling, sweet girl, I would never hurt you. I say these things to help you understand."

She did not want to be this new person.

Cold and collected, methodical, organized, that was her home. Passion and endless emotion were a nightmare. "I don't want to know these things! I don't want to feel these things!"

"I am making you whole, and I will continue to do so, *mon chou*." Abruptly rising to his feet, he stood over her. "I can't have you weeping. I hate to see you afraid. If you don't find a way to calm yourself, I'm going to do to you this morning what I did to you last night. I will make you feel better."

She could not take it again. She could not handle more. "NOOOO!"

Where it came from, the urge to fight him, to bite and scratch, Brenya didn't know. She went mad. The table with their yet uneaten breakfast was knocked over in her struggles, but she never stood a chance against a male so much stronger and faster than she. He had her over his shoulder, dragged her screaming through his rooms, until the mattress met her back and the muscular, great weight of pure Alpha held her down.

He reached to the bedside table, and the buzz of the *unspeakable thing* thrummed before he'd even thrust it inside her.

Voice caught on a gasp, heart in her throat, she felt the pinch of her labia parting, and it began all over.

Inside her skin she was dying, and something else, something alien, was taking over, moving her hips against that intrusion. Sounds came from parted lips that should never have been uttered.

All the while, he held her down, forced her thighs apart, and spoke to her of why this was necessary. "Your body must be assisted to adapt. That way I won't hurt you when you need correction." He fiddled with the edge of the device penetrating her body, altering its programing until it began to expand in her slit. "Right now you need to be reminded that you are safe. You will find relief in submission. Don't fight it."

Was the absolute loss of control worse the second time?

Brenya tried to exist beyond her body, to hold on to anything besides the expansion of sensation and her inability to escape.

The afternoon before in attempting to defend

Annette, Brenya had not won their game. She had not won anything.

Nor had she been punished... According to the Alpha thrusting his machine into her body, this thing he was doing to her was *her prize*.

Less than twenty-four hours ago, Jacques, Commodore of Bernard Dome from whom all orders are issued, had ordered her, his Omega, to take off her clothes right there in the parlor. The door was still closing, Annette and Ancil making their retreat, and Brenya knew they had heard their leader's edict.

She knew Ancil had seen Jacques pull her to her feet, had seen his leader tugging impatiently at the sleeves of her Centrist clothing. Their eyes had met where the door cracked, Ancil standing there for a moment to watch.

Just as he'd watched Jacques rape her in the ventilation duct.

He would have kept watching if Jacques had not growled a warning that another male stood too close.

And then Jacques has kissed her. He had kissed her in such a way she was distracted from all else. It was more than his lips or the starved sounds he'd made. It was his endless touch.

Fingertips smoothed over skin as it was revealed, toying with the feel of it, drawing out tingles that ran from toes to scalp. He sang praises into her flesh, wrote his name upon her. Brenya breathless, her top down and skirt caught about her hips, stood stalk-still while he turned her body against her.

There was no rush in his scheme. Unlike the hours of her half-formed estrous, the Alpha's actions were not directed to alleviate her pain or draw her into immediate pleasure.

They were exploratory. They were gentle—his attempt to perform the perfect distraction to achieve an unseen goal.

In the days Brenya had known the Alpha's hospitality, feeling his hands and mouth on her body had become customary. But there was something different that day.

She was trapped in her mind while her flesh did as it pleased. Only a spectator.

Bit by bit, her body conformed to the Alpha's unspoken will. Her lips would sigh while her brain would scream.

He'd take a nipple to be suckled, her spine would arch... the small Beta voice inside her powerless to make her listen.

Someone else inhabited her body when Jacques played his games.

She was possessed.

And that was why she'd cried over breakfast.

That was why she'd flown into violence when he thought to take her away from herself again.

Because he had a new weapon. A thing he'd slipped inside her and called her *prize*.

What did he call it? The name had sounded scientific, important, nothing like what it should have been called. He'd called it a pliarator. She knew better. It was a mind obliterator.

It slipped in easily enough the day before, so smoothly she wasn't sure what had replaced his fingers, and then it had latched on. Discomfort grew in the form of a muscular ache, distracting, embarrassing, and enticing, Jacques manipulating how the thing sat in her pelvis while she tried to sit up and see what he'd done.

There had been no warning before the buzzing clicked and a soft nodule landed on her clitoris. The vibration had set her to yelp, urged her to press her legs closed against it, and encouraged a pool of slick to gather under her body.

He'd allowed her rebellion because it had made no difference. Even with her legs together, even rolled over on her belly as if she might squirm away, it could not be unseated. Deep inside her body it changed shape again. It stretched her, Brenya keening in pain.

Except, she wasn't sure if it had been pain at all.

A warm hand on her back, the other still fixed to

the device inside the squirming Omega, Jacques smiled. "When an Alpha male chooses to mount an untried Beta female there is a certain protocol that must take place before he can possess her. Had you been optioned for the breeding banks, you would have undergone this practice years ago—just as Annette delighted in these moments with Ancil. Sharing this with you was her idea, and seeing you this way, I can see it was an excellent one. Relax and enjoy."

Mouth agape, sucking in deep pants of air, Brenya stared forward at the distant wall and saw nothing. She could do nothing. Was reduced to nothing.

All by a single pulsating machine.

A machine designed for one purpose: to prepare a Beta female's sex organs to accept the far larger, far more powerful Alpha cock.

The way it squirmed and milked the slick from her tunnel curled her toes. The horrid thing had a life of its own, though she might claw the sheets and fight against its intrusion.

Jacques may have pumped it in and out of her, he may have forced it deeper into her cunt when she tried to push it out, but the robot sensed her struggles and redoubled its attack.

The first orgasm had hurt; the machine had torn the pleasure right out of each nerve.

Immediately it altered its shape, sprang into action when her passage clenched as if to grasp an Alpha knot. Shape bloating, manipulating nerves with shocks, with rotary aggression, it had expanded near the base... and made her groan until drool hung from her lips.

An ocean of slick poured like a river, Jacques no longer pinning her down, but petting and watching where her ass had raised up from the bed and her stuffed cunt was on display as if begging for more.

He adjusted the settings. She convulsed, insides wrenching around the mechanical intrusion as it started its expansion process over again.

Rolling her to her back, he drew her knees to her ears, put his weight on her, and moved his body as if it was his member inside her doing the damage and not some cold machine.

He'd dared to kiss her, to comment on her lust-drugged, blown pupils.

The male had called her beautiful as she lay stupefied and twitching.

When she tried to say his name, tried to beg him to stop, he'd smiled, his head slowly descending between her grotesquely spread thighs. Jacques had lapped at the slick seeping out around the machine as if her sex was the sweetest cream.

"I've never seen a Beta respond to a pliarator as you do. What exceptional creatures Omegas are."

Husky, he'd growled, still savoring her juices. "Imagine it's my cock inside you. When the next knot comes, I want you to feel my seed pulsating in your belly."

As if on cue, the machine began to expand at its base, to fill her up and stretch her even more than the first time. He watched it work her, Jacques seeing to his own satisfaction with rapid jerks of his hand up and down the veined protuberance jutting forth between his legs.

His cock.

She could smell it in her haze, grunted at it like an animal.

The way he abused his organ, how swollen and purple it grew in his fist, the way he practically gnawed her erect clitoris, they both had to be in euphoric pain.

Ready to spurt, he'd reared back on his knees, drew his lips back from his teeth, the muscles standing up in his neck.

The worst had yet to come.

He spoke a command. The machine responded. It opened up, the false knot inside her growing until a hole was made inside her body just the right size to be exploited.

Falling forward to land on his hand, his musculature tight and twitching, Jacques lined up his fat cockhead with her machine spread opening, smeared her tortured cunt with a dribble of his come, and jerked himself in two more rough tugs until pearlescent spray shot forcefully into the space the machine had made inside her.

His usherings were too much for that little pocket, and his seed surged outside her sex, down her crack, in waves of wet heat, over and over until he pulled from her slit to aim instead for her trembling belly.

He overshot, coating her heaving tits, globs landing as far as her parted lips.

When he had crawled over her body, bobbing his pulsating knot in her face, he'd told her to lick him clean… and she had obeyed.

Without question.

Laving him from bulbous base to mushroom tip, collecting the salty taste, slurping, swallowing. With even more vigor than he'd displayed between her legs, Brenya submitted.

In that moment, she did not possess the mental faculty to understand that the Alpha had manipulated his promise.

Jacques had not fucked her. His machine had.

She'd been vanquished like a prisoner, subjugated like a slave, and used like a whore—sore, tired, mindless, and still under the control of his whirring device.

That had been last night, all night.

Even upon waking, her senses had not fully returned, and here he was, forcing her back on the bed to do it to her all over again.

Betas were never reassigned.

He pushed his toy deeper, speaking warmly. "In a week or two, you'll be ready for me, *mon chou.*"

5

Greth Dome

Everything had been prepared, extraction flawless.

Huddled on his lap, her body enveloped by his coat, slept an Omega who was his. The risk of the leap into his arms she'd handled well; the way she'd slept once he had her, a sign she felt safe. Not once had his purr faltered, it projected powerfully, so Claire might continue her rest and Shepherd might take the time to examine his mate.

Her head cradled against his shoulder, he moved a light touch over her face. The bridge of her nose, last he'd seen had been badly broken. While she'd convalesced, doctors had set it, but a sharp eye could see the slight bump and hairline scar. Shepherd traced over the flaw, going next to circle the socket of her eye. That too had healed well, no permanent mark remaining from the orbital fracture, no impairment of vision.

She was in perfect physical health.

A small whimper in sleep, and Claire turned her face toward his chest. It was so like her to be fussy whenever he'd inspected her beauty in the past. Shepherd smirked at her unconscious protest, hugging her to him so he might deeply inhale his Omega's scent.

Across from where Shepherd fawned over his female, a woman read through pages of a chart, quick fingers flipping quietly. "Severe PTSD—improvement nominal. Her list of medications has altered since our last update. Claire O'Donnell is on a great deal of sedatives, some of which are highly addictive."

"She will be given whatever she needs," Shepherd, cautious to keep his voice low, answered the unwelcome interruption.

Dr. Osin looked up from the pages. "There is a list of twice daily opiate injections here, doses larger than what I would deem safe. Considering the cocktail of medications, I cannot foresee the side effects of abruptly ending this *treatment*. Inevitable withdrawal may make her very ill. She will have to be carefully monitored."

He didn't care what she may or may not be addicted to. His Claire probably didn't even know what poison they'd been pumping inside her. None of this was her fault.

The only one in the cargo ship who Shepherd found fault with at this moment was Dr. Osin. Shepherd glared, eyes threatening death, certain the woman's voice was disruptive to Claire's rest. "Leave us."

"As she is still fully medicated, I suggest you mate her the moment she wakes. It will be better to have it over with rather than something she ruminates over. Anticipate fear." The woman stood, spine ramrod as she exited the forward cabin of their transport to join the soldiers in the cockpit.

It had been over a year. Clinically mounting his mate in the cargo hold of a transport ship was not exactly the elegant treatment Claire deserved, but there was wisdom in Dr. Osin's suggestion. It was something Shepherd had already considered himself. And it needed to be done.

Transition would be easier if the bandage were ripped off, so to speak.

A quantity of blankets had been prepared, set in a quasi-nest in case she needed such a comfort. Once he laid her upon it, Shepherd woke her with the growl. Dazed, Claire groaned, half aware when her body automatically responded and slick flowed. The instant he parted the jacket covering her damp nightgown, her eyes went wide and the Omega fully awoke.

Her end of the link frayed, buzzing in panic when an Alpha pressed her down to something soft and held her there under his weight.

"Shhhhhh," Shepherd cooed, trying hard to resonate properly for her so Claire would recognize that he was not going to hurt her. "Spread your legs for me, little one."

It was as Dr. Osin had claimed. Claire was frightened. "Shepherd?"

He placed a kiss on her lips, over her cheeks, moving his mouth to her ear. The Alpha growled again, louder, calling to her to remember what was theirs. More slick dripped, but Claire's breaths were shallow and uneven. Every part of her was tense.

Sex was not going to be pleasant for either of them.

Unzipping his trousers, Shepherd took his member in hand. He was still clothed when his thighs forced hers to open. It wasn't the romantic coupling she deserved, it couldn't be. He lined up. With the initial thrust, looking her right in the eyes, Shepherd found her almost as tight as the first time, and knew without estrous it was uncomfortable for her. For ages he did little more than slowly stretch her, pressing his cock deeper and waiting, stroking and petting, calling her beautiful while she trembled and endured it.

Shepherd knew the secret places of her body, teased and rolled the sensitive nerve bundle atop her sex, all the while speaking to her as one spoke to a frightened animal. It took time, but she grew pliant, the little Omega's pupils blown when she relaxed her pelvic floor and finally let him in.

Bottoming out, Shepherd groaned.

The noise excited her further. The Alpha withdrew, Omega hips followed. It was a gentle rocking, cautious, and only for her pleasure. But pumping into a willing body, feeling her cunt squeeze him so tight —remembering the look on her face as she climbed atop the causeway's safety rail to answer his call— Shepherd could not have loved her more in that moment. He kept her cocooned in his body, brought her to climax, calling out his own long needed release once the knot began to swell and his seed surged deep.

While they were joined, she touched his face as if he could not be real. "They told me you were dead. Why did you make me wait so long?"

He wasn't going to lie to her. "You needed to heal, little one."

Claire began to grow uncomfortable, the knot

something she had not borne in ages. He had to catch her hip and hold her still so she wouldn't harm herself by trying to force out his girth with her squirming.

Staring fixedly at her face, Shepherd watched as sadness overtook her expression. Between the war and their separation, the last few years had been unbearable for her; they had changed her and taken from her.

"They wanted me to accept another Alpha."

Murder was written on Shepherd's face. Silver eyes smoldered, his hips snapped, and the knot was pressed even deeper. "You are mine. No other male will ever touch you."

His anger was reassuring. Shepherd's feeling on the matter absolute.

His Claire held on to it, on to every scrap of true emotion in her mate. "Are they going to come looking for me?"

"No one will look for you." Shepherd nuzzled her cheek, stubble lightly scraping over her skin. "And even if they tried, Thólos is an ocean away. You no longer need to worry over such things."

He knew his Claire didn't want to know the details about her city or people. She did not want to know what he'd done to retrieve her. She knew enough horrible things already.

Green eyes full of fear, wet with unshed tears, her voice broke. "I can't ever go back there."

Shepherd understood. The largeness of his palm cupped her face. He wiped her cheeks as he had done a thousand times before... when she'd been his in the underground den... when he'd kept her safe. "Never."

Encased in the arms of her lost mate, warm, the purr pouring into her, Claire sobbed. "I can't do that again. I can't, Shepherd."

He could hardly bear the torrent of tormented feeling resonating from her end of the link, but he would. He would do it with devout resolution, because he deserved every ounce of pain her sorrow might stir in his breast. "Quiet down, little one. It's over now."

She looked so happy and so heartbroken at once. "I watched you die."

"No, Claire." The tortured look in his eyes was nothing to the sorrow she felt on his end of their link. "I watched you die." Damaged as he was, he'd been able to do nothing *but* watch. He'd watched Jules run toward them, watched his second-in-command administer CPR, the man bleeding from a wound to the torso. He'd laid there as Jules pulled tubing from the med kit hanging from his shoulder and hastily slapped together a direct blood transfusion, the Beta pumping her heart with his fist until he'd passed out.

When the resistance finally found the opportunity to storm into the crumbling Citadel, Claire wasn't breathing, Jules lay pale and unresponsive, and Shepherd... he had to watch as the Thólosen scum dragged his mate away.

If the building had not begun to crumble, they would have finished him. But the ground fiercely rocked, fissures cracking through the marble floors, and they left him there for dead to save themselves.

One or two had even laughed as Shepherd lifted his hand and tried to reach for Claire.

In that moment, he prayed her soul had fled to the Goddess, watching her flop over the shoulder of a man who had no right to touch her.

His vision blurred, death closing in.

"Debris smashed into my roof, you fucking son of a bitch. Everything I'd prepared was ruined!"

Bleary eyed, Shepherd had dared to turn his head, and saw his unlikely savior. Gods he hated her. He hated more that he passed out the instant she tried to move him.

The next time he woke, he lay wrapped in bandages, trapped on the last, stuttering transport ship out of Thólos. And Claire, she was parted from him, in a fortress on a ventilator.

All reports claimed she was too damaged, that

she would not survive—just as his child had not survived. He had raged before the ragged remnants of his men, broken in that cargo hold. Lost in grief, three of them he had condemned to death for abandoning her and saving him. But he could not carry out his intended punishment. Shepherd had been too wounded to move.

Once alone, he'd wept like a child.

But day by day he could feel that Claire hadn't died, she was too stubborn by half—even if the people wanted her blood. While lying savaged in the Premier's Sector, Thólos, her Thólos, had made her into a villain. The very people she'd fought for spat her name as a curse.

Shepherd wanted to hate them, but he could find no room. His hate for Svana was too consuming.

That lying cunt's quick death at Jules' hands had been a mercy she did not deserve.

Reason returned when Shepherd had learned Claire took her first unassisted breath.

And now he had her back in his arms.

His anger at such a memory grew sharp. He knew Claire found the link too much to bear, made himself stop, made his mind blank, and focused only on her.

In a whisper, she confessed, "I don't want to know what was done to get me here."

"All you need to know is that I am taking you

home." Between them, the thread harmonized. Shepherd showed her love. He looked at her as if she were precious, the purr strong.

That was all she needed, that look forever. The knot felt less invasive, the ache in her body bearable. Where her legs shivered from the tension of spreading, she strove to relax them.

Shepherd saw the effort on her end, pleased she was trying. "Sleep, little one. Soon we will be comfortable in our den and our life will begin. You have no need to fear, you'll see."

6

W arm... soft...

The nest was too comfortable to leave. Who would want to leave a place so safe? A place her mate shared, where no one would dare to touch her. The windows' light almost seemed intrusive, a part of Claire longing for the dark and solitude of the underground where she had been safer than she'd realized.

All it had cost her was her freedom and her sense of self.

What good was freedom now?

No, the nest was best. Whatever the bedding was made of she could not say, but it felt like velvet and there was enough to burrow as deep as she wanted. If she was careful, if it was dark enough, and Shepherd was beside her to hold on to, there would be no bad dreams in that nest.

She told herself this, and she lied.

They had arrived only the night before, the pitch black showing her little of her new home. Shepherd carried her because he preferred it, because the nearness of armed and uniformed Alpha strangers made her nervous once they had disembarked from the transport ship. There were gates with high walls, a new Dome that did not smell of rotting flesh.

He took her into a stately fortress; an elevator swept them to the top. There were courtyards, fountains, green things... security, privacy, a mansion if she'd ever seen one. Once inside, Shepherd had to pry her off so he might bathe her, rubbing where her fingers had grown swollen because she'd held him so hard.

The shower was far grander than the one they'd shared before, but Claire noticed little, severely uncomfortable with the idea of Shepherd seeing her naked once he began to tug at her dirty nightgown.

She knew these feelings were foolish.

But she cowered and clung to the fabric. He stopped and removed his own clothing first. He stood before her, stripped bare and still beautiful, the perfect Alpha specimen. But she was sickly, scarred, and she didn't want him to see.

Her reprieve was short lived. Shepherd tugged at

her simple sheath, tore it, giving her no chance to refuse. Once naked, if silver eyes caught where another's cruel nails had marred her skin, if that weighty gaze ran over bites from men who were not her mate or stitch marks from closed incisions, she didn't see. Claire kept her eyes screwed shut, her arms tight around her middle, and she cried.

But then there was warm water washing the smell of the sweat from her hair, warm hands massaging in shampoo just like she remembered, and she grew pliant. The man's understanding of the human body could be a wondrous thing. Shepherd knew where to knead, which bones to press, and just how to draw a hum from a broken Omega.

He was happy. She felt it sing through the link.

She was empty, so she let his emotion fill her up.

Her arm slipped about his waist, her face to his chest so the Alpha could finish a ritual he had always enjoyed.

There had been moments like that in the past that had been theirs no matter what was going on beyond them. In Thólos, Claire had chosen to disregard them, to ignore them out of anger. After Thólos, she had fought to remember each nugget of secret peace, clinging to them like a life raft.

It was surreal to be living it, to stand in the comfort of the shower where there was no need to feel guilt for enjoying warm water over chilled skin.

"I like this."

Shepherd was very pleased. "I can see that, little one."

The shower had been nice; the nest was better. Everything smelled of Shepherd. She could rest there. She was safe.

The usual torture of searching for sleep was driven off by it. He was there, she wasn't lonely. He purred and petted. Nightmares only woke her twice.

That's how she knew it was real. Even with Shepherd there beside her, she was terrified when horrid memories stormed in.

When he asked her about them, she lied.

THE QUESTION of sex was a complicated one. The act of fucking was healthy for Alphas and Omegas, essential to the bond—some would even argue chemically necessary. She had slept almost two days upon arrival, waking only when forced so Shepherd could press her to eat and swallow medication. A firm schedule was important, and he knew Claire had a tendency toward escapism should he not enforce it.

He'd held her, let her sleep, and had not tried to initiate penetration again no matter how hard he was or how much he ached to pump seed into her belly.

She had been skittish, hadn't really enjoyed the first time beyond the compelled orgasm, and needed a reminder that physical pleasure was permissible.

Shepherd gave her forty-eight hours. When her time was up, there was one more daily injection and when she was smiling through the drug's high, Shepherd burrowed under soft covers. She hardly moved. But, when his tongue swiped right between her legs, exactly the way he knew she loved best, his Claire woke with a stifled cry. He delved deeper, lapped and sucked, flicking about inside her as she squirmed.

"You are perfect here."

He gave her no time to think on his words, Shepherd moving to tongue her swelling nub so his fingers might explore where she seeped slick. It was almost easy to gorge himself, swallowing up all she offered, nipping just enough for her thighs to spread obscenely. Over and over he met her eyes, watched her pant for him as her hips jerked. He let her come that way, where she was stuffed full of only his fingers, his tongue frantically licking at her clit.

"Shepherd!"

She had not called his name on the transport ship.

Hearing it drew a growl of approval, a large Alpha prowling over her to urge that sound again. Where she shied, he forced his way, his erection heavy against her thigh. That first taste of her mouth, the flavor of her pussy still on his tongue, was bliss.

He surged in, hips snapping to sheath fully in one swoop. Claire's breath hitched.

He fucked in again. She gasped.

"Touch me, little one."

Her body was twisted, one leg straight, one hooked on Shepherd's arm. She was pinned where they fit together, unable to rock her hips or wriggle away. Green eyes remained locked on the veined rod, seeing it disappear inside her, watching it retreat wet with her fluid. At its base was the bulbous hint of the coming knot.

She didn't move. She stank of fear.

Shepherd took her hand, aware she had not heard him, and put it on his face. "Touch me, little one."

Her attention left his cock to find him excited, silver eyes burning and so very in love. His cheek had been shaved, was smooth under her fingers, the scar in his lips puckered near her thumb. His neck was still thickly muscled, but what caught her attention, what made him hers, were the claiming marks she traced while Shepherd fought himself not to rear and pound harder than her weak body could tolerate.

"Claire, kiss me there."

She wanted to, wanted to scrape her teeth on her mark. She also wanted to run away, to hide.

"You're mine, little one. I'm yours. Bite me as hard as you like. Hurt me if you need to."

A heat grew in her belly, a sense of possession that tightened her cunt and made her want to do all those things. As if Shepherd had read her thoughts, he set her leg free, rewarding good behavior with swirling grinds of his pelvis where friction would only make her croon. The second her teeth locked onto the marks she'd left in his shoulder, Claire came, lapping at the taste of him, breaking skin so she might know the taste of his blood again.

The male roared. Jets of come, the swelling knot, the Omega's back arched and Shepherd cried out like a dying man. Everything inside him wanted to fill her up. Another rush of his seed bathed her insides, Claire so tight around him that for the first time in a year, he felt whole.

His tongue moved to her ear, Shepherd demanding as that last rush of fluid poured from him to fill her up, "Tell me you love me, little one."

Breathless, still clenching around an organ offering pleasure she'd forgotten, Claire panted, "I love you. I've missed you..."

Shepherd kissed her shoulder, peppering the scar he'd given her with affection.

This time, when Claire began to cry, it was not from pain.

While his Omega sobbed, he flipped them over so she might own the position she loved most—so she could rest her ear to his heart while the knot held her tied. So he could tell her things he knew she would not want to hear where she was most comfortable and unable to get away.

"You have a schedule here, Claire, a responsibility to pick up where you left off in your recovery."

He had her in the mating high, he had her drugged on his seed and opiates. He did not have her compliance. "No."

"In the morning hours you'll meet with Dr. Osin."

"No doctors."

"Afternoons may be spent as you wish, but therapy is not an option. I have given your doctor leave to enter this house at will, even this room, should you think to avoid the work you must do. You will find that she is not a woman who will allow you to slack."

Feeling anger toward Shepherd was something far too familiar. It felt right, and it felt ravenous. "You are still a bully, but you have nothing you can force me with now. Who are you going to threaten to kill if I disobey?"

He gripped black tresses tight in his fist, pulling her head back so she might meet his eyes. There was no softness in his words, and no mercy for the sting in her scalp. "I love you, but you need to recover. You cannot live your life hiding in this nest. I won't allow it."

She wanted to make a cutting remark about his hypocrisy, but those eyes held hers and old guilt came instead to make her lip tremble. Memories of Thólos—of grief, loss, pain, and failure, took the steel from her spine.

Claire wilted.

No quarter was given. More commands were issued, Shepherd outlining the life she would have should she recognize all he offered.

7

Bernard Dome

There was a chair nestled in a corner near the bed. A Louis XV, beautifully preserved… a treasure. He'd had it brought into the room the very day he'd seized his Omega off the Beta Sector streets. The amount of time Jacques sat in that chair, the hours upon hours in the dark where he'd watched her sleep…

He knew it was unhealthy.

He knew he was dangerous.

But sitting in that chair was the only barrier, the *only* restraint he could manage when his need raged uncontrolled.

Brenya Perin, Unit 17C, lay sprawled, covered in their combined sweat and fluids, asleep. Had he stayed beside her in the bed, his hands would still be on her, inside her, his mouth unrestrained no matter that he'd pushed her so far she'd passed out... again.

He could not stop himself.

Even after stroking himself to climax, he was hard, his cock throbbing to be buried in her as it had been that first time in the alley. It physically hurt, made him sick to his stomach, and left the muscles jumping in his neck. His sack was so swollen that no amount of self-relief ever lessened the ache.

He held that staff in his hand, squeezing his blasted knot until his vision swam, the last traces of final ejaculation yet to ooze out and dribble down the veined shaft.

It had already been forty-five minutes since she'd screamed under the influence of the pliarator, since he'd painted her mouth in globs of white even as her eyes rolled back in her head.

And he was still hard, still in pain, and still desperately fighting with himself to remain in the chair and only look.

Don't touch...

Grinding teeth, he threw back his head and fought to control himself as another prickling wave washed from base to tip of an angry, denied cock so close to omega cunt.

Leave her be. Let her sleep.

She'd need the rest so that tomorrow she could be focused, so she could come further. She needed the rest so she would feel less afraid.

Every single thing he did, his every breath, frightened the woman soon to be his mate.

There was nothing to be done about that.

Eventually she would know a true estrous, the bond would be forged, and Jacques Bernard, Commodore of Bernard Dome would seal her to him for life. There was no question of his intention. Nothing would change it.

Not a single being under the Dome could challenge his claim. Anyone who so much as whispered of it he'd have killed.

It was easy enough to order a death. Easy enough to keep her under his constant eye.

But it was impossible to tolerate being near her scent, to have her richness layer over every cell in his body and *not fuck her*.

Even now, even under this forced distance, it was all he could think of. Her taste on his tongue was never enough. Twice he had slipped in the dark hours and lapped at her pussy as she'd slept... all the while he had fantasized about doing worse. He'd been so close to testing how much her little body could take after days stretched out by the pliarator, that he'd caught himself already crouched between her thighs, his dick in hand, rubbing it up and down her drenched slip.

He had even begun to push forward... so very close to popping his cockhead past the first tight barrier.

Shaking, breathing so hard he was sure she would hear him, he'd frozen solid. It was wrong. What he'd been about to do was wrong.

Had he woken her that way she would have never forgiven him.

He'd already raped her once. Brutally.

All these thoughts went through his head, but his hips kept pushing forward.

In a panic, he'd flown from the bed, thrown himself into the chair, and jacked off like a grunting savage. The fruitless orgasm did nothing to ease the tension. Knowing that any female in the palace would see to his needs, he'd even considered slipping out into the halls to spend his fluids on the first Beta hole he came across.

But the thought of fucking another was... distasteful now that he knew what true sex should be.

He had made Brenya a promise, yet every day it was getting harder to keep it.

If she did not give in soon, he was going to reach his breaking point and his cultivated façade of control was going to snap.

Fingers in his mouth, he let his tongue play over the taste of her that clung to his skin, imagining her kneeling between his spread knees, those delicate hands running up and down his shaft. He'd train her to relax her jaw enough to take him into her mouth. In time she'd learn to swallow his girth down her throat like a practiced Beta slut.

She would swallow every last drop of come he gave her. All of it. *He'd make her*.

Snapping up his head, Jacques opened his eyes and made himself look at the dreaming female. Thoughts of a darker nature were the reason he was failing in this endeavor. He had to control himself. She was a person. She was his love, his *mon chou*, who needed to be coddled, cuddled, cared for, and cherished through her difficult transition.

She would be more than a wife.

He may have fucked every last Beta in Central, he may have used them just as they had used him in their foolish attempts to grab for power. He'd tossed them all aside after a night. Brenya was not one of them. She was more than a warm body. More than the most delicious cunt he had ever tasted.

She was his mate. He was king, he deserved the perfect queen.

He forced his hand from his cock, took his fingers from his mouth, and made both hands grip the delicate chair's armrests.

Deep breath in. Deep breath out.

This was how he spent his night hours.

Under his breath, he whispered into the shadows, "I need to fuck you, Brenya. I need to fuck you before I hurt you."

In time, he'd even adjust her to his proclivities. She would learn to adjust to his *tastes*.

Just as she was learning pleasure, despite reluctance, was powerful and all consuming.

"Just one more day." He'd said this night after night, like an addict taking one day at a time. "One more day and you'll be ready."

Jacques knew it was a lie... she would not be ready until estrous. She could not be with all her mind was processing, the new hormones, the mood swings, the fear.

He'd grown skilled at lying to himself. Standing from the chair, his cock finally laying down, he moved to the bed to take her in his arms for sleep. "One more day."

She slept best crushed beneath him. She slept best trapped completely by his body. And he, he had never known more tormenting or peaceful rest in his life.

~

Stirring with a groan, Brenya woke uncomfortable. Tension in her neck, her shoulders, her whole body had gone beyond what could be easily ignored. Too much had been done to her, her musculature rebelling and then reveling in the sweeping shocks that bowed her back off the bed when Jacques played.

As if the man lying at her side understood her grainy complaint, a warm hand slipped to her neck and began to rub.

It felt good enough, that she dared to whisper, "I don't think I can take any more."

He pressed a kiss to her shoulder, and began to pinch his way down her spine, one vertebrae at a time. "A hot bath will relax you."

There had been no dinner yesterday, no breakfast the day before. Something had come over the Commodore since the introduction of his pliarator, and he'd hardly let her out of bed.

Though she had not even bathed in days, that could wait.

She had learned speaking seldom led to the outcome she desired, but Brenya's stomach was rumbling and she was desperate. "I am very hungry. Any food will do, even the pastries. Can I please eat something before... anything else?"

"You're hungry?" The male raised himself to an elbow and hovered over her submissive recoiling.

He took in the state of her expression, the tone of her skin, her eyes, and answered as if her hunger had never occurred to him. "Of course you're hungry. Food shall be ordered at once, anything you want."

He was daring her to ask for Beta rations, and Brenya comprehended that if she did, food would not be coming... not until he'd corrected her to behave as an Omega should. "You choose and I will eat it."

"Other females are always desperate for anything granted by their Commodore. They would have requested their favorite cuisine, something that would have challenged the chefs. Something expensive." He was still in a moment of self-reflection, his eyes stormy as if some internal argument was being lost. "You never ask for anything."

That was untrue. She had asked often for him to stop. "I am very hungry."

His eyes grew untrusting.

Angering him never worked out well for her. Brenya immediately apologized. "I'm sorry."

His weight came down upon her, lips setting a kiss at her hairline. "I would give you anything you desired."

It twisted her feelings when he made such outrageous claims, and before she could stop herself, frustration darkened her features. "All I am asking for is food. If you continue this way, I won't last much longer. Please, I'm hungry. Let me out of the bed, and let me eat."

The Commodore reared back to his knees, unabashedly naked over her, and stared down as if she had burned him. "I'm going to leave the room, Brenya. Food will be brought into the parlor immediately for you. Eat as much as you like."

He kept her feeling as if at any moment she might slip off the edge to her doom. She'd rather fall down the side of the Dome day in and day out than set off the male narrowing his eyes at her when she backed toward the headboard. "Please... I need food and water."

His powerful thighs flexed, the Alpha backing off of the bed with his half-mast erection bobbing between them. "Of course. Wine too perhaps? Champagne? Shall I have Annette come to keep you company? You ladies amuse yourselves while I attend to state business."

Jacques turned to a door Brenya had yet to see him open, an office of sorts. Without preamble the door closed, the sound of a lock turning like the *click click click* of clock cogs grinding together.

Dumbfounded, her fingers fisted in dirty sheets, Brenya stared at the door waiting for it to be thrown open. He would come back and force her down. He would spread her legs and dive his tongue into her body while saying things like, '*You are better than any breakfast. I could feast all day*'.

And then he would, while she grew too distracted by sex to remember her body's requirements.

It was a test. It had to be. If she stepped a toe out of the nest, he'd rush in and make her stay.

But an almost instant delicious smell assaulted her nose. In the direction of the parlor was what he'd said would wait. Food.

A cramp set her stomach growling as she sat on the mattress and warred with herself on what to do.

"Brenya?" her name was called. Not by a male, not with a warning edge to it. It was called from across the apartments in the soft lilt of a polished female.

She still could not make herself move, and Annette found her that way—sitting naked and wide-eyed in bed, hair a nest of tangles, unwashed and reeking of Alpha attention.

Exposed breasts bruised, nipples chapped and ruddy, Brenya didn't think to cover herself… all she could think of was how thirsty she was, how much she wanted to eat whatever was waiting.

"My god…" The Beta female's composure quickly returned, Annette smiling like an angel as she offered a hand and said, "Come here, Brenya. It's okay. I'm going to take care of you."

Watching the perfectly coiffed woman in her clean dress, breathing hard yet feeling almost dead inside, a matching pair of silent tears fell from Brenya's eyes. "I am so hungry."

"Well, you're in luck." Annette seemed breathless, her arm reaching out earnestly toward the Omega. "There is food enough for an army waiting for you. Come now, let's eat breakfast."

Wet honey eyes darted to the door Jacques was behind, Brenya unmoving.

"He's not coming back, Brenya."

Next, Brenya's gaze cut to the sunny balcony where the overturned table and broken china still littered the ground. The food wasted all those mornings ago rotted, untouched. Annette followed her line of sight and promised, "I'll have that cleaned up. It will be as if it never happened."

There was a flood of thoughts all racing to the forefront of Brenya's mind, crashing into each other until one won out. "Did you know that Betas are never reassigned? Centrists kill them. I'll never go back to Beta Sector. I'll never make *the descent* again. For the rest of my life I will be trapped inside the Dome."

A small hand came to take the sheet and wrapped it around the shaking woman, Annette's voice low as if they might be overheard. "I know exactly how you feel."

8

"You must learn to distract him and guide his urges. It is never wise to allow Alpha males free rein of their thoughts." A warm pass of dripping cloth crested Brenya's shoulder, Annette taking great pains to clean the woman sitting silent in a tub of steaming water. "For example, before Jacques grows too focused on *a physical objective*, ask him questions off topic. His lot are generally so vain that any conversation about themselves is never resisted."

Nudity in front of another female was completely natural to Brenya. Her Corps had bathed together, used the facilities together, ate, lived, slept together, her entire life. Males and their groupings were the same. It was easy to submit to Annette's good intentions. It was easy to be grateful that the Beta had fed her, had let her swallow glass upon glass of water, had ordered a bath, and washed her bruised skin with care. "You do this to Ancil?"

Annette snickered, dunking her hand into the water to saturate the washcloth. "Of course I do! Asking Ancil about his day buys me at least an hour before he remembers to mate me. If I compliment him while he speaks, two hours. Some days he just gets hungry and forgets sex all together until bedtime. By then, I'm less concerned about him spoiling my hair or dress."

Sleepy from a full belly and the weightlessness of her body in so much water, Brenya yawned. "When you ask him to stop, does he stop?"

Annette paused, and an awkward silence grew between them. "They never stop, dear. But, they can be redirected. Alphas have all the power, Brenya. Even in my marriage contract I am bound to perform... not that I have ever complained. But, I have heard of other wives less content in their match."

She turned, water sloshing the side of the tub when Brenya asked, "What do these wives do?"

The pretty blonde held her eye, her serene expression slipping. "I don't know. That is why you must heed my advice. Distract him, chat with him, ask questions. Keep Jacques talking. When that has run its course, finish him quickly before he gets *creative*. Rub his back afterward, make him tired."

"Finish him?"

A blonde brow cocked. "You must understand the fundamentals of sex? Didn't anyone teach you such things when you were younger?"

There was a simple protocol to scheduled pleasurable coitus sessions. George had petitioned, she had agreed, and she had done as instructed by Oversight. "You lay still until they finish. Afterward you return to your duties."

Annette stared, unblinking, her mouth unable to catch up with her mind. "Well, you see, Centrist females are educated a bit differently. We are encouraged to enjoy ourselves, both with a partner and alone."

Who would like such mindlessness overtaking their bodies? "Enjoy what?"

"Has he never made you... you know? Jacques has a reputation for being a very thorough lover. Women go to great lengths to get into his bed."

"Why?"

Eyes sad, Annette set down the cloth and sighed. "Someone should have explained these things to you. Jacques should have known."

Their comfortable morning was beginning to sour, Brenya frustrated. "What things? The horrible machine you gave him? He steals my mind away until I'm nothing but a body he controls. That machine... that *thing* is always inside me. When I tell him no, he smiles. He holds me down if I fight. He increases the sensation if I behave. There is no stopping him!"

"I suggested the pliarator so you would not get hurt again... I never thought you'd dislike it." Guilt brought dampness to the Beta's eyes. "I'm sorry."

Thinking of that machine was already doing something to the place between Brenya's legs. The water hid the effect, but slick had begun to gather. "When he uses it, I am not able to speak to distract him. Your advice won't save me."

Annette sobered from her selfish tears and tried to explain. "If you do not submit to the pliarator, the next time he... makes love to you, you will feel pain. Can you not just make yourself bear it out of self-preservation and the greater good? He's the Commodore, Brenya. I can't... you can't..." At a loss for words, Annette muttered, "Nothing can be done."

"You mentioned women who want this attention. Could they not take him?"

"He has never been faithful to a lover. The fact he's not cast his eyes toward another in all these weeks is a miracle. But, you are Omega and he seems to enjoy being out of his element. Maybe if you acted more like the other females do, he would tire of you."

None of her questions seemed to lead to worthwhile answers. "What do they do?"

"They fawn on him, seduce. Smile when he comes in the room. Touch him. Seek to give him pleasure in bed. And by that I mean, do not lay there, do not fight. Stroke him. Compliment his... size." Annette made herself busy with washing Brenya's arms, seemingly unsure of what to properly say. "There are other options to wear him out until we can come up with something."

But the male never got tired, or hungry, or thirsty. He never stopped. "How will I do these things if he holds me down?"

There was a hidden determination in the Beta, anger toward Jacques Annette didn't try to hide. "Alphas enjoy chasing their prey. Do not give him a reason to hunt you. If you went up to him the moment you see him later, got on your knees, and took his member in your mouth, you would have all the power. You would catch him off guard. Don't run, don't fight. It's not working. Mimic all his other women, and he might grow bored."

Anything. Brenya would try anything. "What do I do once it's in my mouth?"

～

ANNETTE HAD TRIMMED Brenya's hair into a different shape, put paint on her eyes, pinkened her lips and left her in a dress. The angry red scar pinching her cheek had even been muted with flesh colored paste.

She looked like a Centrist Beta, doe-eyed and poised.

They had practiced smiling, topics of conversation, how to nod when another person talked to reflect engagement.

Just as Annette had said, the bedroom had been cleaned, the terrace remade into a quaint sitting area in the sun. All around, the air was still tinged with Alpha scent, but the offensive nest was fresh.

It was as if the last weeks had never happened.

Except the marks of Jacques enthusiasm were hidden under Brenya's white dress.

Soon enough, Jacques would return.

And when he did, Brenya was going to hold her hands tight behind her so the Alpha could not see them shaking, and smile. She was going to walk up to him. Then she was going to ask about his day, offer him tea, repeat the things he said back to him. If that didn't work…

If that didn't work, she was going to touch him as if she wanted to, exactly as Annette had described. She was going to *finish him* before he might take off her dress.

With Annette at her side, they had shared a quiet afternoon—the Beta woman composing a letter, Brenya napping on a divan near a fine view of the city.

To spend a day doing nothing for the sake of pleasure was uncustomary. By this hour, Brenya would have walked outside the Dome, made repairs, written her log, walked back to Beta Sector, showered, attended to her duties in the barracks. Instead she had spent the day sleeping while Annette hummed softly to her belly.

When she wasn't dreaming of jasmine, Brenya watched the Beta.

She was so composed, so sure of herself in all she did. She had no qualms about calling a servant to bring them some lunch or to order an errand.

Brenya could emulate the woman, copy the way she sat, the way she spoke, her laugh and smile and never come close to the elegance. If all Centrist women were this way, the sole Omega was doomed to be forever awkward.

She was asleep again when the male barged in, awake in an instant and sitting up alert to the stink of aggression. Brenya did not remember to smile. Everything she had practiced went out the window with one look at the Alpha's rage.

Ancil had his hands on Annette, already having

dragged his wife from her seat as he roared, "What did you do?"

The woman, the composed woman who had been so kind to her, stood shocked by her husband's display. "What on earth do you mean?"

He gave the woman a hard enough shake that her hair fell loose from its twist. "Do not play coy with me. I know your games and tricks. Your note arrived while we were still in session... and can you guess what happened, dear wife?"

All innocence, Annette answered as if there was no threat. "Our Commodore asked for a report and I gave him one."

"*Your Commodore* picked up his chair and smashed it into the wall in the middle of a sensitive trade negotiation. I have been winning Jacques over for weeks before he found his disfigured Omega, had practically earned his agreement. Greth Dome's offer expires tonight; their cargo ship is already turning around. Do you have any idea what you've done? What you have ruined for me?"

"I have no idea what you're talking ab—"

Right there, with Brenya braced in her chair, the Alpha struck his pregnant wife. The slap landed with force enough to knock the fair blonde's head to the side.

Pressing her hand to her red cheek, staring wide-eyed at her husband as if looking at a stranger,

Annette whispered, "He cannot be trusted to take care of her. He forgot to feed her for days, darling. He deserved the words on that page."

"If he chooses to use her up until she dies, that is none of your concern. Your sole purpose is to carry my son to term, not dishonor my house with your pathetic meddling. Do not doubt Jacques might have you killed... if there is anything left of you by the time I'm done."

Shaking her head, tears running down her face, Annette whimpered, "He would never."

Ancil grew before her, his grip distorting the flesh of the Beta's arms. "You do not know him so well as you think. You are certainly not valuable to him beyond serving as a dimwitted babysitter to his toy. Prepare yourself to learn what his anger looks like, but first you will deal with mine. When I am finished with you, you will remember your place." The male began to drag her to the parlor door, bellowing, "You will pay for everything I lost today!"

Brenya didn't know when she'd stood or how Ancil's embroidered coat ended up in her fists. But she held on to the man dragging away a terrified woman, grunting from the effort to stop him.

Her whole life had been an exercise in physical training. She'd climbed the outside of the Dome daily for years, labored with heavy equipment.

Annette might have been delicate, with soft arms and skin. Brenya was not.

But she was much weaker than a hissing male Alpha—one who shoved her so hard she fell back to the floor, her newly sculpted nails having ripped off in his coat.

Before the door might slam and Annette was to be hauled off, Ancil turned and showed his teeth. "You will take off that ridiculous dress she put you in. Ready yourself on the bed, and when your Commodore returns, you will beg him to fuck you. If I learn you have not, I will make her pay for it."

9

B lood trickling down his nose, a bright bruise blooming under one eye, Jacques stood before the mirror and waved off a Beta attendant ready to blot his monarch's face clean. After the sparring he had endured, he was in no mood to be touched by anyone.

Except Brenya.

But should she see him so battered, it might startle the Omega. So, something had to be done before he returned to their apartments.

White linen wet with cold water soothed the cut on his lip. It was the only thing cold water soothed. His quick rinse had done nothing to battle the erection even hours of physical exertion had yet to diminish.

Five Alpha males had been summoned to spar against him.

Five, because the Commodore of Bernard Dome wanted to feel pain.

He needed the penitence; he needed his body to be a reflection of hers.

In her letter, Annette had described in detail what he'd ignored in the rut. Annette had outlined every last way in which he was killing his mate.

Bruises, bite marks, starvation, dehydration.

She had called the most powerful male on the continent powerless over himself—accused him of a complete lack of control in the presence of his lover. Every word was correct.

Even now, even with pulped flesh and sore muscles, his thoughts circled on how tight Brenya had been when he'd callously rutted the Omega in the streets.

Her pain had been his ultimate pleasure.

The guilt had come later.

And it had come hard.

Guilt was not a powerful enough motivator to a man who always got what he desired. He could force her at any time. In fact, he was starting to think that he should. Whatever damage was done to keep her safe from his needs would all be erased the instant his pairbond tied her soul to his.

Ancil had made a strong point. Rape her now if need be, make her like it and call it what he will.

Do what had to be done so rational thought won the day—so that his Cabinet did not see him this way and presume to find their leader weak. Do it before someone used this weakness against him.

Would she scream or cry? Would he be able to care when her cunt was spasming around his cock?

How much of his soul would be forfeit once the knot formed and the copious seed engorging his balls forced its way into her belly. Could he live with himself?

Yes.

Yes, he could, and he knew it.

Behind him, his security advisor, one of the most influential men under the Dome and his longtime comrade, watched his every move. Ancil's dark hair had already been brushed and braided back into the rope required by all ranked Alphas. His skin had been oiled, his wounds tended by a pretty Beta attendant. That same attendant was now bent over the locker room's bench, his ass stuffed full of Ancil's cock.

Pleasure was the heart of Centrist culture, using a nameless Beta attendant, male or female, this way normal. Before Brenya, the pair of them had even made a game of it.

It was a game Ancil was tempting him with now.

The Alpha was making low throat noises with each forward thrust, stretching open the soft, hairless young male who braced.

Ancil would work the boy's cock with one hand, in a slow steady rhythm. He would get that Beta organ swollen and ready to burst, only to squeeze his fingers around the base, fuck in harder, and deny the attendant release.

This they had done side by side many times, the ultimate goal, to see how hard the attendant might spray his come once the knot pressed the Beta's prostate. Whoever could get them to shoot farther won.

In this case, Jacques had already waved off the attendant who could have served his needs. So, Ancil had thought to tempt him by working up his Beta's moans, making sure the pretty male's throat was open and ready to choke down an Alpha cock.

They could share him. There could be relief.

Jacques didn't know when he'd turned from the mirror to observe, was hardly aware of how swollen his cock was or the constant drizzle of pre-come leaking from his crown. Transfixed, he watched Ancil grow rough with his toy, heard the slapping of the male's groin against the soft cheeks of the Beta... took in the grimace of pleasure the Alpha wore as he threw back his head and just took what was his.

That was not the scene Jacques saw. He saw Brenya bent over the bench, her legs splayed and ass up as he pounded into her.

She, like the Beta, would have her mouth hanging open. She, like the Beta, would brace and make low mewing sounds.

When she came, she would cry out, milk his cock dry, and be forced to submit, stuffed full throughout the duration of his knot... her belly bulging a little more from each accumulative blast of ejaculate trapped behind the knot.

The Omega would be completely at his mercy, unable to stop or run from whatever part of her his hands wanted to explore.

Her ass... he'd stretch that sweet pucker with his fingers and show her what pleasure could be had there. Knotted, caught in the mating high, he'd finger that hole. Someday, he'd fuck her there.

The pliarator was not just for stretching cunts.

How many women had he shared with Ancil over the years, pushing the female body to the limits of pleasure and pain with two knots and the occasional third cock down her throat? It was a pretty picture to see Brenya in his thoughts that way... and then it wasn't.

The concept of sharing her was... infuriating.

He'd seen the way Ancil looked at her. His security advisor was biding his time for the invitation to taste Omega.

Sudden wrath abruptly ended the daydream.

No Alpha but he would ever touch her.

That in itself was a problem... and yet another reason Jacques was considering moving against his best judgment toward the Greth situation.

His mate would be coveted; his power already was. No one was infallible and no friend really existed at court.

Breathless, watching Ancil's every last muscle tense as he orgasmed, Jacques said, "Contact the Greth Queen's Consort. Tell Chancellor O'Donnell we will accept his trade agreement. His ship may land."

BRENYA PERIN WAS beyond the door, secured by no less than seven Alpha guards. It did not seem enough for something so fragile and so priceless. The helmets shielding them from Central's environment and preventing the scent of nearby Omega from teasing their nostrils reflected back the approach of their unsmiling Commodore.

He did not ask for a report. He did not look at a

single one of them. Jacques' thoughts and flesh were devoted to a single mindedness.

Things could not be allowed to proceed as they had. He had done wrong here indulging her fears, in letting the lion play the kitten. He had done wrong believing patience was the cure.

Facts were facts. He was an Alpha; she was his Omega. Order had to be established and domination enforced.

He had given her all the power, an unstable female, and in doing so, had harmed her.

So he would treat her like a slave, guide her in what was expected from an Omega, and adore her all the while. The rest he would teach her... later.

Pushing through the door, he found the foyer dim. She was not in it, did not come to properly greet him as a good wife should.

"Brenya Perin." Gruff, cold, he managed to speak her name without the whine of a dog in pain entering his voice. His cock twitched, balls so heavy with unshed ejaculate they throbbed miserably. "Brenya Perin, come here at once."

There was no sound in return, no shuffling of feet. No answer.

A scratch of irritation sharpened his gaze. No one disobeyed him. This poor behavior he had fostered by coddling her and begging for her attention. Too many smiles he'd wasted, too many longing looks.

That was at an end.

"Brenya Perin!"

Still nothing.

Tearing at the collar of his shirt, he rejoiced that it was anger pumping through his veins and not insatiable desire. It would give him something to hold on to when she received her first punishment. It would give him focus before he fell at her feet and begged her to love him.

Plodding through the foyer, the parlor, throwing open doors he found more darkness and quiet.

There was one last place she could be. His bedroom.

Perfect. He would not have to drag her far to the nest. It would be done quicker, and then his Omega would be told *exactly* what was expected of her from now on.

Unlike the rest of his apartments, the lights were softly glowing, showing just enough to betray his errant guest's whereabouts…

Her head was turned away from him, and though he could not see her face, he knew her eyes were unblinking and focused. On her hands and knees, naked, her thighs parted just enough that her pink slit became the center of attention.

He'd held her legs spread open enough times to

know every last detail of that perfect place. The inner labia peeking out of soft outer lips, the warm, wet pussy that could drip the sweetest honey.

She held that position, a suggestive statue that lacked the scent of her male on her skin.

She was presenting the only way she knew how.

The lie of control failed. Jacques forgot his anger, why he was there, who he was. His entire being came down to the meat hanging between his legs. A tear of fabric, and his member was in his hands, his slacks hanging open, zipper ruined.

Noises were coming from his throat like those of a vicious animal and they made his prey tense… and also excited her. He could smell as much, feel the traces of slick in the rushed seconds it took him to surge forward and prod that slit with the swollen head of his dripping cock. It was a blur, a sloppy entrance to a place not quite ready and yet on offer.

Shoving his way inside, he took her hips in a harsh grip that would prevent any thoughts of resistance. He fell over her back and set his teeth to a tense shoulder.

Inside she felt like velvet, lacking the abundant slick he demanded. That was set right with a guttural growl and more force.

Halfway.

Halfway buried in tight Omega cunt, fully out of his mind, and dangerous. His hand found her hair, yanked her throat back and bowed her body. He could see her face, the dilation of her eyes, and the fear.

"Submit."

She could not nod. She could hardly maintain her position under his attack, her wide honey eyes locked on his.

Frustrated that her channel revolted and grew unyielding at his order, he pulled out enough to leverage his weight, and slammed back in. "You brought this on yourself."

Her lashes lowered when he hilted, a shaking breath passing her lips.

The animal pounded away, the beast inside him folding her down so the Omega's cheek was flush to the bed. It was graceless, disgusting, loud, and violent.

Glorious.

This moment was the epitome of the word *fuck*.

The Omega's noises, her muffled grunts under the force of his hips fed his need. They were not the sounds of pleasure, but the whimperings of surrender.

He had waited so long to feel her encase his cock, long enough that he was going to exact every last ounce of pleasure from the mating that he could. But her insides began to flutter, and his hands began to shake. Rhythmic squeezing of the female's impending orgasm moved up his shaft, coaxing the beginnings of a knot.

The basest part of him, the animal, wanted to rage at the little body that was his to use as long as he wished. His greater urge was to shout out at the blissful pain of so much repressed ejaculate gathering up for the first eruption.

Unable to pump his hips, mindlessly trying to force the expanding knot deeper, Jacques roared.

Her timid orgasm was twisted up into his until it surpassed her ability to bite back her shrieks.

The Alpha wrung it out of her, just as her pussy milked his cock for everything the Omega feared.

His mind did not clear from her panting into the sheets, or at seeing the blood from the scratches he'd left on her back. The beast under his skin wasn't done, fiddling with her this way and that while the knot persisted and his orgasm continued.

The usherings, ten maybe twenty times over the course of his knot, drew up his balls, scratching at his spine to spurt down the satiated length of his cock as each one possessed him. He squeezed her with each one, growled should she think to move or resist.

Sometime later he woke from the madness, found her lying limp, staring vacantly forward under his weight.

He brushed back her hair, satisfied and eager to

cuddle his prize. "It won't always be this way. I will learn to be gentle with you despite my need, *mon chou.*"

Blinking once, Brenya murmured, "You must tell Ancil I obeyed his order. Please don't let him harm Annette further."

10

"What?"

There were still tremors in her belly, Brenya unsure if they came from her or that thing with its repetitive bursts of fluid still jammed inside her.

It was done. The *little death* had taken her. An Alpha knot had been made to fit inside her.

And yet she was alive, her racing heart proof her body persisted.

"I asked you a question, Brenya. Why would you say that?" He seemed startled… perhaps even gravely disappointed?

Turning her chin as far as her neck might allow, she viewed him over her shoulder, saw the damage done to his face, and asked, "Did Ancil strike you as well?"

Tone hard and deadly deep, Jacques demanded, "Did Ancil lay his hands on you?"

She put her cheek back to the mattress and sighed. "He was so angry when he took Annette away. He hit her, threatened her. I tried to stop him. After they were gone I worked up the courage to follow, but there are many Alphas blocking the door."

The sounds of his irritation grew. "You are not restricted to these rooms, Brenya. You may explore Central at any time you wish, so long as your guard accompanies you. They are there to keep you safe."

"I waited for hours…" A wave of sadness deadened her voice. "There was nothing else I could do to help her. So, please, contact him and tell him I obeyed. Don't have her terminated because of the letter. I need to know she's safe."

He ignored her less than subtle accusation that he might have his childhood friend killed, assuring, "Annette is in no danger, I promise you that. Her father is the Finance Secretary and her mother Matron of the Arts. They would take Ancil to court over the smallest of infractions. Furthermore, Ancil has been in physical training with me for the last several hours." Jacques spoke softly, brushing his fingertips back and forth over her cheek. "You see, Annette went into labor. She'll be separated from him until her son is born and kept in confinement for weeks afterward."

None of his soft spoken replies lessened her anxiety. "And then? What's to stop him from hurting her then? Please tell him immediately that I submitted... tell him I begged you."

The male sighed, his breath warm on her ear. "Ancil has a way of motivating people to the outcomes he desires. The Dome is his first priority, his duty. Your reticence and my indulgence of your fears had unbalanced the powers that be, putting us all in danger. His actions in inspiring your complicity... were unscrupulous, but it is done now. It would be best not to mention it."

Jacques tried to explain it away, to justify an Alpha's brutality toward his pregnant wife, and it made Brenya feel cold and completely unsafe. "He used me. He used her... terrorized her." It was the only word she could think of, but not nearly the castigation deserved. "Centrists are *bad*."

"Politics are complicated and seldom pretty. Annette understands, someday you will too." Tightening his arms around her, the male swore, "I would never strike you in anger, Brenya."

His knot was still in her and she wanted it out. She wanted whatever he had spilled inside her washed away. When the base of his cock started to contract and a river of their fluids rushed from her,

Brenya let out a sigh of relief, then a squeal of revulsion when Jacques scooped it into his palm and held it to her lips.

"Drink it."

Don't run. Don't fight him. Maybe he'll grow bored.

Parting her lips, Brenya heeded Annette's advice and swallowed the sweet mixture down. When he pulled out and rolled her to her back, when he began to massage his semen into her belly and mound, she submitted. When he told her he loved her and that he would always take care of her, she nodded as if in agreement.

And then he held her tight, and she did find a trace of comfort in his strength... until he grew hard again and took her face to face, eyes open, watching her as he conquered her body and bent it to his whims.

It was a smooth entry, the male focused on her reaction. When her lips parted on a quick intake of air as he pressed in deep, he praised her. When a tiny coo left her throat at his slow, rolling retreat, he called her beautiful.

In and out, slow and easy.

There was slick enough from when he had fucked her from behind, so much under her hips that the wet noises of their joining blended with sighs to make obscene music. He was on his knees between her spread legs, her body in view and angled so he might tempt the hidden nerves of her sex like a true lecher.

He knew how to draw out her need, how to stoke it and tease. Rolling a tight nipple between forefinger and thumb, Jacques could make her come. Tapping her clit in an uneven rhythm distracting enough to confuse the senses, make her insides squirm, but holding her just short of release.

When he took her by the neck, lightly wrapping his fingers around the front of her throat, something in Brenya faded far away.

The new Brenya came forward, gripping the wrist of her Alpha as her hips bucked. She was so close, so very close to forgetting why the beautiful male pleasuring her was *bad*.

A part of her psyche whispered to her that even though it was his hands on her throat, she had all the power. She could make him come at will, force his body to satisfy her.

Her eyes traveled from his smirking face, over a muscled chest, a defined torso, to where his jutting length eased in and out of her body. The veins throbbed at its base in preparation of a new knot. To see it begin, to know that menacing, bulbous organ would jam deep inside her and keep them locked sent her over the edge.

She came, tightening her cunt to the point the

male had no choice but to respond. Expanding knot pushed past her opening, the Alpha grimaced, unable to hold back sounds of ecstasy.

They were in harmony, the mating high's influence total.

Wrapping her ankles around his waist, she pulled his hips closer, angled her pelvis to stimulate the place inside her that refused to stop pulsating, and took every drop of semen her body might squeeze from his.

He fought to speak past his release, the fingers around her neck fluttering before he might squeeze too tight. "Good girl. You, my dear Brenya, are a very good girl."

He pet her through the extended length of the knot, eased her into sleep, and woke her by licking the used place between her legs clean.

And then he took her again.

THE GRETH TRANSPORT ship landed while Commodore Jacques Bernard was indisposed. A blue-eyed Beta stepped from the gangplank to be greeted by Bernard Dome's Security Advisor, the Commodore's Cabinet a distance off. When those persons offered by Greth Dome in trade descended behind the Ambassador, Ancil took a deep breath, forgetting all protocol to step forward and seize a pretty black-haired female. A moment later, the Security Advisor raced inside the palace, an estrous high Omega in his arms.

The Beta Ambassador in question stood composed despite the tableau.

He introduced himself as Jules Havel, Ambassador of Queen Svana and her mate Chancellor O'Donnell.

11

Greth Dome

W hat once had been a grim bunker was now light-drenched rooms, spacious, each corner filled with items Claire was certain Shepherd had little to no interest in— unless he saw her interest. If she touched something, he seemed to memorize the movement, looking to see if she admired or disliked.

In this *home*, there was a rotation of experiences, objects, sensations… crafted environments.

Those first days, things vanished, paintings on the walls replaced, or a rug shifted so subtly she wasn't sure if she'd imagined it. A chair was added near a window she preferred to stand beside. Flower-filled urns waited by the bath, bright and fragrant and so very different than the blooms she'd seen in Thólos.

She didn't understand the effort behind Shepherd's silent undertaking. Mostly it made her feel like a bug in a jar, the way he watched, the way he read into every breath she took.

Unsure if he was waiting for some confirmation of effort, she thought to appease him. Claire ran a hand over the Oriental rug she lounged on. "This is very pretty."

She wasn't facing him, could not see his reaction to her words, and wondered why she didn't turn her head.

Her last hour had been spent flipping through an item he had never allowed her before: a personal COMscreen. She was learning of Greth Dome... or at least learning of the things Shepherd had prepared for her attention and education.

The language was unknown to her, translations listed beside bright stories, entertaining bits of cultural information, a catalogue of local art, of fashion, of food.

As she read, she could feel his eyes on the back of her head—feel the way he leaned on the link to see inside her.

"You are very pretty, little one. Much prettier than the rug."

On that point, they would have to disagree. She

may have been pretty once. A great deal of surgery and scars had changed that. The worst damage was hidden by her clothing, but under her dress, they were still there.

They would always be there.

She wished he'd stop acting like he could not see them. It was not natural for Shepherd to be so... blind.

If she shifted back an inch or two, her head could rest on his knee. She could touch him and forget how she felt. She could take his feelings as her own and forget.

Claire was tempted, knowing he'd immediately thread his fingers in her hair. But that was not what Shepherd wanted; he wanted her to look at him.

He didn't need to say it. She could feel it.

Hesitating, her attention turned to the window instead. The sun was setting. It had been a beautiful day: her private veranda full of plants, a tall wall surrounding *her garden. Her house. Her things.* That's what Shepherd called them. But they were all too foreign to feel like they belonged to her.

It was too much like the North Wing with its paned windows, paneled walls, and fine furnishings —with its regiment, and medications.

This home was an anomaly, one where she never saw another soul aside from Shepherd. Whoever cleaned, whoever tended the restocking necessities, Claire could only imagine. Her meals were still prepared by some unseen chef, and brought to her by her mate. Rich food, with heavy sauces, just like he'd fed her when he'd stolen her from the Citadel—when she'd been hardly more than bones. As if their ritual had never altered, he sat with her as she ate, only now, he talked to her.

Shepherd had adapted, curbing his need to force compliance to instead coerce by asking questions. "Why won't you look at me, Claire?"

The purr, the stroke down her hair, and Claire felt her lips form a smile before stifled emotions caught up.

Peeking over her shoulder, turning to rest her cheek on his knee, she gave Shepherd all her attention. Green eyes, soft, ran over the man—his pressed shirt, starched slacks, clean shaven cheek. It was ironic to see him dressed so *formally*. She stroked his ankle, feeling the wool socks and polished shoes, remembering a time he'd only ever worn combat boots. "I should paint you again."

The way the skin beside his eyes crinkled set her heart racing.

"If you like."

Draping herself against a thick leg, Claire hummed. "I could paint you with my eyes closed."

"I have seen photographs of your bedroom wall

within the North Wing." His finger traced over her lips. "I was very flattered, little one."

The memorial wall papered with watercolors of silver eyes in every expression beside her bed, mention of it took her smile away. An imagining of her dead son had been on that wall.

The man sitting on the fine couch purred louder. Not only because of the sharp stab of sorrow that altered her expression, but because there was something at his end of the link he was trying to conceal from her.

Shepherd remained steady while she was still unstable. He did everything in his power to maintain a front, but she could see the gnawing guilt scratched on his soul. Even more, she felt the memory of his intense loneliness.

She had mourned, and he had borne it from this great distance, all the while building this new life for her.

"Was it hard for you?" She wasn't sure why she'd asked. She was not sure she wanted to know.

He frowned, agitated even if offering a stoic exterior. "Being separated from you was necessary. You required extreme medical attention I could not provide, nor would you have survived the flight. I did what was best for you no matter my"—he seemed at a loss to find the word—"discomfort."

Claire understood. Shepherd had sacrificed his

wellbeing. He'd had only a strained link, and it had been his turn to relentlessly pace—as she had once paced—because he had to so he might keep from going mad in this fine house.

Had he heard her voice? In moments of madness, had he searched room to room as if he might find her?

Did he dream of her every night, or had he suffered nightmares as she did? Had his years in the Undercroft seemed a haven in comparison?

The Omega nestled closer, shut her eyes so she might enjoy the tug of his fingers in her hair.

She was supposed to be happy now. She was supposed to pretend. This house was hers. Outside was a verdant terrace garden surrounded by high walls waiting for her admiration. Green dresses he'd chosen hung in her closet. Rooms full of distractions waiting to tempt her.

She could play the contented kitten, and she did. But in moments like these, she did her best not to meet his eyes. Her acting was abysmal, and they both knew it.

The silver saw everything: his skeletal mate, the dark marks under her eyes, the way her hands shook. He saw further than nails she'd chewed to stubs. And still he pretended not to see her scars.

It's like he wanted to only look at her, and not the history written on her skin.

Claire knew what he was about. In Thólos, he'd manipulated and forced her into physical health. He thought to do it again. Maybe his will was strong enough to achieve his goal.

Hers was not.

"You want me to tell you I love you," Claire sighed against his thigh, knowing how to soothe the sharp concern Shepherd tried, and failed, to hide in the bond. "I do."

"Do you?" Reaching down, Shepherd pulled her to fit on his lap, a pleased growl offered when she nosed his neck. "Clever little one, do not think I'll let you off with flattery and sweet words. You promised to walk with me outside. Don't nap too long."

12

Nestled deep under the covers, Claire woke alone. She knew that if she stepped out of the nest, if she tiptoed to the window, she would find him. Whatever mess she had made of the garden the previous day, he tried to repair while she slept, uprooting plants she'd over-pruned and replacing them, as if his mate wouldn't notice.

It was sweet, in Shepherd's strange way. It was also true that if he didn't put in the *secret* effort, everything would have died weeks ago.

Once, she had once told him she wanted a garden, windows too.

Now she had both.

He had made his own promises, ones she wanted nothing to do with: a grand new world.

Claire, what happened in Thólos?

It was the same question every day. This grand new world, if it even existed, was unknown to her. Much of the last year within the North Wing was a blur, what happened before a nightmare, and its toll had been taken.

She wasn't Claire O'Donnell anymore.

The venue had changed from North Wing to Greth Dome, but the schedule remained the same: medication, therapy, painting, music.

A beautiful piano was downstairs, a black grand she could play in the sunlight while surrounded by a view of beautiful plants. But she was only allowed to play after she answered the question: *what happened in Thólos?*

Everyone around her knew what had happened in Thólos. Dr. Osin knew. Though Claire had never seen her there, the old woman's accent was her own.

It was insulting that she had to sit across from the unwelcome female and face that question morning, noon, and night.

Her psychiatrist's hair was almost white, steely, her form wiry and strong. There was nothing soft about Dr. Osin—she was a Follower, after all. One, Claire was certain, must resent the assignment of tending to their leader's broken mate.

"What happened in Thólos, Claire?"

"A lot of people died."

"Who killed them?"

"I did."

"Because of this?" A flyer bearing her naked image, aged and creased, was slid across the coffee table between them.

Claire didn't want to touch it, was certain she was going to be sick. "I hate Thólos." Her throat was tight, the space behind her eyes burned. "I don't want to talk about it anymore."

Dr. Osin never cut her slack. "What happened in Thólos, Claire?"

That question made her heart clench, it made the thought of food horrid. Anxiety, panic—more than the sedatives could manage—would hit her hard every single time she heard it.

She had to give an answer or the doctor would keep asking. She had to offer something or the torment would continue.

Small voice replied, "Nothing good happened in Thólos."

The notepad was set aside. "We will continue tomorrow."

But it wasn't just tomorrow, it was every day.

Claire pulled the covers from her head, unwilling to lie there any longer. The comfort of the nest was not enough if Shepherd was not in it to cuddle with. The only safe place to be was wherever he was.

There were walls around her new home—walls within walls within walls. So many, she could walk outside and be assured no one would bother her, that she was safe.

Shepherd's grand new world...

How he maintained this position, she did not know. There were no sounds of war under the Dome. There was no stench of death, no pop of bullets.

The people who lived here had let them in. Claire had not seen one of them. Though it was weak on her part, she didn't want to think about it.

It was easier to pretend it was only the two of them... Dr. Osin's intrusions aside.

Pulling on a robe the same shade of green as the weeping trees which grew in the surrounding garden, Claire crept down the stairs, pulled open the door, and went to him. Shepherd had known she was coming. Though he stood away from the flowers, the telltale grit was still under his fingernails when she interlaced their fingers.

"Where are your shoes, little one?"

The question brought a sleepy smile, Claire leaning against his arm to watch the sunrise. "Would you like me to make you breakfast?"

He was purring, her worries forgotten at the sound of it. "I would. And then we walk."

She'd grown to enjoy their walks, just the two of

them around the compound's private perimeter. There was even a segment right against the Dome's glass. She could trail her fingers on it, see the condensation collecting outside. Beyond the glass there was no snow.

Outside sat mountains, a great river... growing things.

Everything around her was a reminder that life flourished.

In order for that life to continue to flourish, it had to be fed. Her newest job was to feed her mate.

The venture was interesting, gave her a chance to share something with him each morning that she had been denied underground: domestic normality. Shepherd's breakfast was simple. One big blender filled with stinking mold powder, raw eggs, nut butter, and whatever else he needed to supplement his altered system. Making it for him wasn't a chore. Claire would put in a little cinnamon, or cocoa, but she was certain it still tasted awful, teasing him about his *one restriction*.

He would suck it down in huge gulps, Claire making a point of not staring, while she gathered her small meal. She didn't like to eat much in the morning—he knew that now—usually a boiled egg, toast, and some coffee. Medication was next, waiting on the counter between them. Shepherd would watch her poke at the AM set, already presorted for her by another: antidepressants, antipsychotics, sedatives, a heat suppressant, a vitamin.

Seeing the assortment made her unhappy. She didn't show it, but it was always there in the link.

Her regimen had been tailored within Thólos' North Wing and watched with a hawk's eye by Dr. Osin now that she lived in Greth. Even though there had been no major meltdowns in the short months since Shepherd had brought her home, there was still so much to swallow.

Claire always took the little blue pill first, before she ate a bite. The rest were portioned as her meal progressed. Vitamin last.

"I love you, Claire O'Donnell."

Green eyes stopped brooding on the Monday-Sunday medication container to look at the man across the counter. There was a band on his left ring finger; she now wore one too. "O'Donnell isn't my name any longer, Shepherd."

Though he was purring, his answer was curt. "I never had a surname, you know that."

"If you are only Shepherd, then I am only Claire. I'll take the nothing at the end."

Large fingers stroked her jaw. "What of our future children, only Claire?"

And just like that, the moment was ruined. She

fought to keep her food down, to keep herself from
breaking things.

What happened in Thólos, Claire?

For just a moment, she looked up at Shepherd...
and hated him.

THEY MISSED their walk that day, Shepherd far more
focused on fucking his despondent mate back into a
state of tranquility. He had to be careful. There were
rules now, because others had hurt her. He couldn't
take her from behind. She had to be able to see him
so she might not panic, might not be in a position to
suffer a flashback.

Aggression had to be severely moderated.

Shepherd still made certain to enforce his domination, because that's what she needed when she
was scared, angry, or lost.

The first time they'd joined after reuniting, she'd
been terrified. It wasn't fear of Shepherd, it was just
the unlanced poison stuck inside her from everything she'd survived and all that had been taken
from her. After waking in the new nest—after the
rules were broadcasted—he'd mounted her again,
over and over, until she'd fallen into a dreamless
sleep, voice hoarse from crying out his name.

Shepherd did not let her out of his sight for even

a moment the first weeks. The routine deviated little from what had been theirs in the Thólos underground. If he could be inside her, he was. She hardly stepped outside, though she could if she wished to.

Claire had a studio to paint in, a COMscreen should she wish to read, and had been told—more times than she could count—that all she had to do was ask for something and it would be acquired.

"Are there other Omegas here?"

Shepherd was dead serious. "Would you like me to procure some?"

Her lip twitched. "Are you going to round up friends for me?"

"There is a team in place to see to your recovery and companionship. It can be augmented with Omegas if you need them."

"No, Shepherd. You can't just *procure* Omegas. That would not make me happy. It would make me angry." A year, and in the most fundamental ways he hadn't changed at all. Claire hesitated to ask, "What about the Omegas… from back home? The ones your men took as mates?"

The way the Alpha looked at her, Claire was not certain if he was intrigued she had asked after the females or angered. "Those who betrayed you will never be allowed near again. I would not even allow them to step foot in this palace. They are with their mates in another sector, they are not allowed free rein of the city. In a year or two my stance may be reconsidered."

Palace?

She should have known better. After chewing her lip, she asked, "Are they well?"

"They are settled, content. Several have children."

The conversation was over, Shepherd having used the one word that was guaranteed to shut her down. Before she could slip back into her medicated daze, Shepherd pushed a little more, "Would you like proof of my claim? Do you want assurance that they are happy?"

"No." Maybe... "I believe you."

"The children could be brought here."

"You can't separate babies from their mothers!" She was awake again and very angry he would even suggest such a thing. "Swear to me you won't."

Large arms crossed over his chest, Shepherd challenging, "Their fathers could escort them so you might meet them, but, yes, the mothers would be left behind."

"Asking your men to come here so I can see their offspring is ridiculous."

"I do not ask my Followers. I order and they obey." Shepherd stepped closer, menacing. "Do you understand that, Claire? I could demand anything, anything at all, and they are bound to do it. You like children. You could learn their names, paint pictures for them."

He was annoying her with his grandiosity. "You make yourself sound like a king—"

Shepherd growled, "I am greater than a king. Or have you forgotten? I brought ruin to the most corrupt city on the planet. It was easy…"

The words fell heavy on a dumb tongue. "Thólos still stands."

"Limping and fractured. Those who survived have less than five years before famine and exposure kills them all. My point was made greater that way, so the lesson might continue for the world to see. And believe me, the world is watching."

Claire didn't even know what to do with his words, because there was something dark in the link she must not acknowledge. "Svana destroyed Thólos. It was all her doing."

Shepherd made sure Claire heard every word. "Everything that was done was my machinations, my leadership."

She felt as if she'd been punched in the gut. "I was there. She did it."

"You can't pretend I am something I am not for the sake of your comforting delusion. I ruled Thólos; I now rule Greth. Under this Dome, I hold the position far more firmly than any before me. No one can challenge my authority. Those who could were removed. Claire, I crippled Thólos. Its citizens are rotting as we speak, and I will enjoy knowing that city suffers insidious harm until my dying breath. But I *did* leave it uninfected, enjoying the show of their scrambling pleas for mercy to other Domes who ignore them or face my wrath. I will assure other nations will avoid them, that they will refuse to buoy the infrastructure as it collapses. That city will be hell on earth no matter how loud they beg."

She could feel a river of tears fall down her cheeks. "Why are you saying this?"

"Because I love you."

Had they not been in the confines of their kitchen, the whole Palace would have heard her shriek. "I can't hear this! I don't want to talk about Thólos!"

"Don't be a coward, Claire. Fight me."

It felt like she was walking the ice again, cracks spreading out under her feet. "I told you I couldn't do that... I won't stand for Thólos. That part of me died."

"You know they deserve every torment they will feel."

"What's left was what you made! There was good there once. YOU ARE KILLING ME."

"The only good thing that ever was in Thólos is standing before me, very much alive," Shepherd growled, stepping nearer should she think to run before his lecture was complete. "And she doesn't belong to Thólos anymore. She belongs to me, to my domain, Greth Dome. She belongs in this palace that I have secured for her. She belongs on the throne at my side because I have made her queen."

She ignored a goodly portion of what he said, her thoughts on one man. "Corday was good."

The second it was said, Claire wished she hadn't spoken. Fear hit her hard. "Corday is still alive right? You didn't kill him when you came for me, did you? Oh my god, Shepherd, please tell me you didn't!"

"He lives." The giant's fists were clenched tight, his silver eyes burning. "Don't think I wasn't tempted... until I saw what he's become."

There was something deeper going on, the real reason Shepherd was orchestrating his attack. "Explain?"

"He hates his people, himself... the world." Shepherd watched her confusion, watched her try to process something seemingly absurd. "It's a legacy I understand."

Claire knew him better than that. "Corday is gentle, he's sweet. I don't believe you."

Shepherd sounded almost proud. "The Undercroft has that effect on the soul."

"What do you think you're doing?" Claire

ground her teeth, angry, so angry. "Why are you saying these things?"

He repeated his reason from before. "Because I love you."

"…and you want me to not love my friend? You can't share my affection with those who cared for me when I was alone and scared?"

"He is not what he was, little one. *That* is my point." Shepherd stood taller, took her chin so she was forced to look. "The fall of Thólos brought out the true heart of everyone. Do not be fooled by his smiles or the flowers he brought you. That goodness was corrupted when you were ra—"

Her hands flew to her ears, Claire breathing too hard to see straight. "SHUT UP!"

One swipe and the dress was ripped off, a hard cock shoved in with only the kitchen counter digging into her back to offer support. Clawing and scratching, she raged at the Alpha, punishing him with bites as he thrust.

Holding her bare ass in his hands, yanking her body back down when she squirmed away, Shepherd grunted like a beast, barely able to form the words, "Fight me, little one. Remember."

The initial aggression was all hers, Claire so far gone she hardly noticed how she screamed when all the rage inside her squeezed, cracked, and dumped out like stagnant filth. The power of her release, she sobbed through it while the violent Alpha used her as he had not since Thólos.

Just when he was about to knot, he spun her around, bent Claire over and plunged in from behind. The knot expanded, her legs kicking while Shepherd roared, "This is your Alpha, your mate! That is who is fucking you!"

Dangling from her awkward position, feeling the cramp of her orgasm milk Shepherd's cock, she understood. Living in seclusion, where they walked trails and enjoyed one another, didn't change what he was, or what she was. He needed her to accept all of him, and not pretend while they played house.

He was never going to be easy on her.

There would never be a day he'd regret forcing her into a pair bond. It was the only way he would have ever won the female's affections. His *reward* was perfect, dominating her body and mind sublime to such a man.

Shepherd twisted her hair in his fist, pulling her neck up so he might dig his nose in and sniff, so his grating purrs would be felt best with her back to his chest. "You are my little one. Sweet and so pretty. The way you come around my cock is something that I hunger for, hearing you scream for me my favorite sound. You are *my* wife, *my* mate. No time apart could change that. No courting Beta, no estrous, no drugs. You didn't want me, I know that. I enjoyed the challenge. I enjoyed stealing your affection. I enjoyed mating you into oblivion more times than I can count. I'd never let you go. EVER!"

Claire could see his reflection in the window, could see that the man knotting her was Shepherd and not a horrible memory, and wondered if he'd plotted the entire conversation just to reach that moment, knowing she would have that reflection should she need it.

Her breath fogged the black marble under her cheek, Shepherd petting her face as he continued his tirade—all of it so she could hear his voice and be still. He kept her there through the entirety of the knot, gauging each fleeting expression.

He'd manipulated her.

She knew it.

There was a flaw in the story he'd told to draw out her anger. "Corday would not turn on his people."

Shepherd growled softly in her ear, "Don't fight the knot, little one. Stop bearing down."

Claire had not noticed her body's rejection and drew a deep breath to regain control. "The counter is cold."

A reassuring stroke warmed her from hip to shoulder.

In the glow of rough orgasm, her tension melted. "You can be a real prick sometimes, Shepherd."

The purr magnified, cuddly Alpha monster settling over her. "Tell me that you love me."

"I love you." Claire sighed. "Don't speak ill of Corday."

Shepherd ground his hips against her rear, the Alpha purring, "I know a man full of rage when I see one. Another year or two, and he would make a good Follower."

"Why tell me these things?"

"Because I love you."

13

Bernard Dome

"You must forgive me for failing to greet you upon your arrival, Ambassador Havel." Jacques had not dared bring the foreigner to his private apartments, choosing instead to meet with the Beta in the grandest palace sitting room. Cherubs cartwheeled overhead in a fresco that rumor suggested had been transported from the Vatican before the Dome was sealed. The furnishings were solid gold and rich light warmed the walls. It was a beautiful place where the Commodore had ordered the deaths of many rivals over the years. It was a room in which he'd killed seven of them personally. It was a room perfect for the coming conversation.

Before him stood a Beta with a muscular neck for his dynamic. A wise man would assume that under the ambassador's clothes was the body of a conditioned soldier, that he was potentially dangerous... that he had been chosen not for his diplomatic abilities alone. Much could be hidden by a good tailor and a careful barbering. The male's close-cropped beard was immaculate, his brown hair short, tidy. Even his nails had been buffed. But when their hands met, calluses hardened the Beta's palms, saying much while disclosing nothing.

"It is I who owe you the apology. I should have notified you that Lucia was on the cusp of estrous. Considering your lack of Omegas here, I should have anticipated the ecstatic outcome of your man. May their newly forged pair-bond gratify them both." Though his remark was fluently spoken in French, the words were clipped by a harsher accent. And even with his expression settled into a passive genteelness, Jules Havel lacked a smile.

Jacques' shark smile was big enough for both of them. "The remaining females have been put away... out of enthusiastic reach until I decide what is to be done with them."

"Of course. You must choose one for yourself. I had extensive dossiers prepared listing talents, traits, personality, family trees. Each lady is remarkable in her own way. There was a great deal of competition to be chosen to live in the beautiful Bernard Dome."

And be mated to the most powerful males where they would live a life of spoiled luxury... or serve as spies.

"Greth must be rich in Omegas indeed. I have heard rumors that even your queen is Omega."

Jules did not answer, choosing instead to turn his attention to the leather bound folder under his arm. "Her Majesty extends her personal greetings."

Jacques refused the offered letter. "And Chancellor O'Donnell? Is that what he's calling himself now?"

A dark eyebrow arched, Jules stone cold. "Would you prefer to know him as Shepherd? There is no need for us to pretend that Bernard Dome doesn't control the functioning satellite systems and has some grasp of what happened in Thólos. The most dangerous man in the world knows you're watching. He's watching you too."

Bluntness was seldom employed in Centrist society, yet greatly appreciated by the Commodore who'd rather not spend weeks on niceties and persuasion. "And sent you across the globe's largest ocean to trade ten Omegas for orange trees..."

Hands folded at his back, Jules approached the window to look out over the beauty of the European city. "We possess the ships you lack. We have an entire ruin to loot for resources, making us capable of building anything we desire and going where we please. Bernard Dome's stores are finite. We could change that. Shepherd is not looking for war. The war was won and it is over. Now he is looking for allies."

"Against whom?"

Vibrant blue eyes cut across the room and seemed to look straight through Jacques. "Time. Inevitability."

Jacques crossed an ankle over his knee, sitting back in his chair to ask, "Why orange trees?"

Jules' expression did not betray the direction of his thoughts. "Our queen is very fond of them, and he is fond of pleasing her. It is the only thing he's fond of. I suggest you remember that when dealing with him."

THE BRUISING on her wrists was beginning to fade, her health returning now that Jacques made a point of seeing she was fed regularly. Now that he was free to fuck her, his demeanor had greatly changed. He still seduced her at his whim, but he also doted... at least that's the word he used.

Lavish meals, long baths that always ended with him penetrating her under the water.

Most days he left her alone for a few hours here and there to attend state business. When he returned, after he fucked her, he would invite her to play games, talk, ask a million questions she could not answer.

Sometimes he'd rub her feet. Sometimes he'd tell her to get down on her knees.

He liked to be rough, would make himself be gentle. And each new mating left her with new marks—a roadmap of where he'd been.

Brenya looked at the latest scuffs marking her knees, remembering a time when bruises were common but earned in a different sort of labor.

She missed fiddling with the mechanics of broken infrastructure, she missed being useful to the Dome. Now… what? She was left with little to do but dissect an ancient bedside clock while Jacques was away. Spread before her on a table nearest the window with the best light lay the cogs, dials, springs, the weighted pendulum, all the inner workings that when put in the perfect order, functioned seamlessly.

She could take it apart, put it together. Take it apart, put it together, over and over, and every piece would function seamlessly. It would always work so long as each component did their job. As she had done her job as a Beta.

Unit 17C had been a cog in the Bernard Dome machine.

Knowing that now, knowing how Centrist Alphas regarded the Beta workers, troubled her. All that effort, the peace of her previous life, the cohesion, what did it matter here? Was it okay that Betas lived so completely removed from the realities of the Dome?

Yes. They were safe that way.

Central was dangerous. Alphas were dangerous.

Brenya was beginning to suspect that Jacques was the most dangerous of all.

Look what he'd already done to her.

After that first night he'd penetrated and knotted her, he'd held her close and assigned her duties: perform for him sexually, bend over at his whim, learn the tricks that any Centrist female already knew. In return, he would cherish her with bruises and fluids, with ecstatic moans and orgasms.

When estrous came, he would teach her to love him. All would be well. Trust in your Commodore. Obey.

She was still a cog. A cog who knew things she wished she didn't.

Even the most menial engineering task had been more fulfilling than whoredom.

But was she a whore when the anticipation of his return had... marked the soft chair where she sat? There was little he had to do to prepare her body now. A rich purr when he set eyes on her and her underthings were ruined.

If he growled, slick dripped down her leg.

In her weeks in Jacques' care, he'd trained her well enough.

Well enough that she knew he would not be pleased to find his clock in pieces. Still she took it apart every time he left, fingering the bits as if they held the answers she lacked.

It was always completely sound before he returned, back on the bedside table and ticking softly.

There was nothing she could not take apart and put back together. What did that matter now?

Serve the Dome with advanced skills, or learn to suck Alpha cock practicing exactly how to squeeze a knot in your hands as a male shot gobs of sperm down your throat.

That she had yet to master, choking both times he'd drawn her head to his lap.

Absently her fingers went about their business, rebuilding the clock because it was almost time for the Commodore to return.

Setting the clock back in its home and tucking away the *tools* she'd used to take the thing apart: a nail file and a pilfered fork. She smoothed her skirt just in time to hear the click of the door.

She was supposed to greet him in the foyer, even pretend to smile just as Annette had practiced with her. She was supposed to put her hands on him, maybe press a kiss to his cheek.

These things she had tried, and each day performed better.

He had his arms open. Her body would fit there, tucked against him while he might kiss the top of her head and say hello. Sometimes it was nice.

If she closed her eyes hard enough as he murmured to her, it wasn't so bad.

All she had to do was think of jasmine.

Turning her nose into his chest, Brenya inhaled deeply. She could practically smell the sweet flowers. In fact, all of him was drenched in sweetness.

She froze.

He smelled of other females.

But not of Betas.

Dumbstruck, Brenya backed away and tried to analyze the strange feeling in her stomach. When her rigging had failed and she'd plummeted down the side of the Dome, the same feeling had wreaked havoc on her gut. "I don't understand."

Jacques took pity on her desperate look, and explained, "Three days ago a transport ship from Greth Dome landed. Ten Omegas have been offered citizenship so long as they are mated to Alphas of my choosing. Today I was introduced to the women. Interviews were conducted so I might get to know them better."

Real Omegas, here? Real Omegas who knew how to be Omegas, who weren't... what had Ancil called her? Disfigured?

Hand creeping up to her cheek to hide her worst flaw, Brenya swallowed, completely at a loss. "Am I to be reassigned?" Terminated... was she to be terminated?

"No." Jacques reached forward to pull her palm from her cheek, leaning down to kiss the long scar that pulled down her lower eyelid and puckered the flesh into an unseemly Y. "You are to be adored, by me. Forever."

Blinking, breathless for reasons she could not comprehend, she took another step away. "I feel strange."

The Alpha's purr took on a tenor close to the roar of an engine, loud and pronounced. When he crooked his fingers and she failed to come to him, he made no hesitation of moving to take her.

She did not resist, thoughts whirring. In fact, she hardly paid attention to anything he was doing.

For once, he was not trying to fuck her. There were no fingers slipping under her skirt, or wet kisses placed on her skin. Jacques was only rocking her, whispering nonsense as he purred and held her on his lap.

Deep down she knew that if he stopped, she was going to cry.

And that confused her more than anything.

14

Saliva was dripping in a long string from her chin, his Brenya's face red and eyes watering. He held her face down longer than he should, always a touch too rough, but unable to control himself when her throat spasmed into choking gags around his cock.

She made the most beautiful noises of desperation.

With an extended groan, he threw his head back and shot this first and largest burst of come straight down her esophagus. Her arm flailed and her back bowed beautifully just in time for another mouthful.

She may have only learned to suck cock a week ago, but Gods there was no one better.

Letting her up for air, Jacques watched as she panted around the fat crown of his head. She knew not to let it slip from her lips, that he'd want to feel her tongue and even the slight scrape of her teeth while she fought to breathe. Because he was going right back down that raw throat once the second wave of his orgasm hit.

Ten times they would repeat this, twenty. If she could make it through his whole knot there was always a great reward.

Fist tangled in her hair, he grimaced, pulling her back down to fuck her skull as another large rush shot down her throat.

She almost threw up on him.

He loved that.

Loved all the more how rich the air was with her excitement. His naughty Omega could not hide such a plentiful reaction. She was dripping slick; no doubt it was running in rivulets down her bared thighs to mark the carpet.

"Be a good girl. Suck it down."

Knots never persisted long without the rhythmic spasms of Omega pussy to squeeze the blood vessels properly. She might have her grip wrapped around him, she might be trying to do as ordered, but he'd be coming less than ten more minutes.

Which meant he'd be hard in twenty and fucking her like she deserved in her cute little nest.

He had not told her what her new habit of arranging pillows might mean. He had not whispered in her ear that her need to have the bed made in a certain way was adorable to him beyond all measure. Such talk made her shy.

But she was more Omega day by day.

Certainly more vocal.

Their life together had improved innumerably since the evening he found her presenting on the bed.

Was Jacques to be furious at Ancil for interfering, or grateful his comrade was made to be the villain, when, in fact, he had been determined to force his way inside her one way or another that night? Was he to laud his friend for creating such a clever scenario, or hate him for terrifying his female?

Either way, it had saved Jacques from once again earning the title of rapist. Brenya never need know about what could have been.

She gave a wet cough and he showed her a moment's mercy.

Drool shined both her chin and the throbbing mass of his cock. He was undone, one fist caught up in her hair, his other hand gently stroking her pink cheek. "Does your Alpha's come taste good? Is that why you're licking it all up?"

Her little tongue was slavering over his slit, licking clean any escaped drop just like he'd trained her to. Or had he taught her *that*?

"Answer me, Omega."

His use of her designation instead of a name seemed to disrupt her performance. Brenya went still, jaw slack around his girth. Just in time for him to force her head down and shoot another round of sperm into her belly.

She took him smoothly as he whined out such pleasure. Her throat did not struggle, nor did she fight for air. She just lay bent forward, still and blinking. For that he made her hold him longer than he would have had she protested.

Raising his hand, he ended the game, leaving his cock jammed down her throat. She would have to disengage of her own will... her occasional distant behavior never encouraged.

It was some time before she put her hands to his thighs and drew back.

His knot was already fading.

Aggravated for reasons he could not pin, Jacques asked, "Trying to drown yourself?"

She didn't answer, rolling back on her heels. Dress split down the front so he might fondle her beautiful breasts, hair mussed and face slimy from their sport, she looked to the carpet and seemed lost.

He took her chin, raising her eyes to meet his. Jacques smiled at her. "I want you to show up at dinner like this. Oh, how I'd love to parade you before them so perfect and so freshly used."

When she shook her head no, he chuckled and amended, "But, of course, then they would want you more than they already do. Since I am greedy, you must be made presentable." Using his thumb to wipe her wet lips, he asked, "How was the first course?"

He knew her jaw must ache, that her throat burned, and her eyes were swollen from choking. He also knew that some part of her liked it very much. He'd guide her to embrace that part.

They were going to be so happy.

Brenya's answer was honest. She was always honest. "Your body tastes different than George's. Better. I am still hungry though."

He hated the reminder that she'd been with other men, aware his jealousy was hypocritical considering the hundreds of men and women he'd fucked. "It is impolite to mention former lovers when in the company of your mate."

From the passing confusion on her face, Jacques was certain her thoughts were tripping over the concept of her tech being her lover. She almost seemed ready to argue before thinking better of it. Instead, she muttered, "I would appreciate some water."

Slacks open, softening cock proudly displayed, Jacques smirked and reached for a nearby glass. He held it up to her lips, enjoying that she knew better than to try to take it from his hand. When she had swallowed enough, he pulled it away, wiping her chin with his fingers.

Purring, Jacques licked his lips. "There is something I wanted to try with you, something I think you're ready for."

Unfolding from the ground, Brenya's fingers went to the buttons of her dress, the Omega acting as if she had not heard him. "I'd like to go visit Annette. It's been many days, and I've never seen a baby before."

But she was dripping slick. A good Alpha must see to her needs first. "Now?"

Wrecked, but smoothing her hair as if it might help, Brenya softly added, "There isn't much time before your formal dinner... and it would make me happy. I imagine babies are very interesting."

She'd said just the thing to tempt him to consider. "You want to hold a baby?"

"I have not seen Annette since..." There was something like anger in her eyes, an emotion an untried courtier like Brenya could not hide. "I'd like to see Annette."

Setting ankle to knee, Jacques sighed. "I ordered her presence at dinner this evening so she might keep you company while my cabinet entertains the Greth Ambassador."

His mate's disappointment was obvious. "And the baby?"

He relented. "Shower first, then go visit your friend. I'm certain Annette will be glad of your attention."

There was a brief sparkle before Brenya turned to trot off toward the bathroom. A beam. Perhaps the first genuine one outside of sex he'd witnessed— which didn't exactly make him feel better about all the tight smiles she'd been giving him at the door. Calling after her, the man said, "Don't take apart any of her clocks."

The Omega froze so suddenly she almost tripped. When he saw her hang her head before she disappeared to shower, Jacques wished he had not teased her. But, it was better that she understood.

Under his breath, he muttered to the empty room, "That's right, *mon chou*. I'm always watching."

"JACQUES TOLD me these were an appropriate gift. I hope he was correct." Arms weighted with a bouquet of fragrant flowers almost as large as she was, Brenya dipped down to show their beauty to the woman resting back upon a mountain of pillows.

The blonde smiled, her skin pale as she

motioned for an attendant to gather and prepare the gift. "It is so good to see you, Brenya. You're the first to visit since I was placed in confinement..." Annette winked. "You must have powerful friends to get past that door."

But it had been many days since the baby had come. "What of Ancil?"

Voice cracking, Annette whispered. "I've been told he's indisposed. He has yet to see his son."

The concept of parenthood was foreign to Brenya. Those chosen for the breeding bank did not keep the child after early weaning, if at all. She was not even sure if males were aware offspring existed. Uncertain what to say, she sat on the edge of the bed and peeked into the nearby bassinet.

The baby inside was awake and wiggling in his wrappings. He looked like a cherub version of his angel mother.

Gently touching a foot, Brenya marveled. "He's so small."

A tired chuckle preceded, "Matthieu didn't feel so small on the way out."

Now that Brenya knew was abnormal. All Beta women asked to participate in procreation were told delivery was conducted painlessly while they slept. Several of the women in her Corps had undergone the procedure.

Hesitation led to awkward silence before

Annette said, "It was on Ancil's order. In the last minute, he demanded a natural birth for his heir."

An heir he had yet to visit...

The medical room was full of light, decorated so as to give the impression of a boudoir. It was nothing like the med station in Beta sector. When the attendant returned and set the crystal vase of flowers beside the bed, it was hard to see anything but beauty. Yet it would seem it had been Annette's prison.

She didn't know if it was the right thing to say, but Brenya felt she had to offer something. "He promised me you would be safe... after I did what Ancil ordered. Jacques promised me."

Considering the way the attendant was watching their every word, Brenya was certain both Alphas would hear a report of all that was said—though, now she suspected Jacques was most likely watching by other means. "If he lied, I would never do it willingly again."

"Dear, Brenya." A pale hand fell to her much darker one, Annette forcing a soft smile as if she held a great horrible secret. "You were beautiful that day you know, in the white dress with your hair curled. It's a pity Jacques was denied what we had planned. I think he would have preferred you coming to the door as you were, all innocence and smiles. You had a wonderful surprise prepared for him."

After the way he'd torn his clothes in his rush to cross the room and slam inside her, Brenya doubted it. "It only hurt a little."

Letting out a deep breath, Annette lay back and stared at the ceiling. "I suppose I could say the same. He didn't even leave a bruise."

"I don't like your husband." It had come unbidden and with venom that tasted bitter on Brenya's tongue.

Almost dreamy, Annette answered, "I am not the greatest fan of him at the moment either. But I do love him, Brenya. I love him so much it hurts. I know he must love me too."

It was genuine, even Brenya's shy smile. "Who could resist loving you?"

15

When Jacques appeared before her, he was already dressed. The style of clothes was as strange as any she'd seen, but that was not the reason she stared at the broad shoulders filling his white jacket.

His long hair was free of the plait, waving and golden around his unfairly handsome face. These were not qualities she would have noticed weeks ago. Just as weeks ago, she would not have looked in the mirror and paid attention to her own features.

How many times in life had she considered the color of her hair?

Never. She had never cared that it was light brown, or that her eyes were light brown, or that her skin was light brown. Appearance did not matter; accomplishments did.

Yet seeing him so beautiful, she felt like a glob of mud beside a statue of gold.

Annette was decidedly attractive. Even Ancil with his feline features and mean looks had the grace of a prime Alpha. None held a candle to Jacques. No matter the Commodore's selfishness or abuses of power, he was breathtaking and he knew it.

And she? She was not.

Without Annette and her box of paints to make her pretty, there was only so much that could be done. It was up to Jacques, who took great delight in zipping her into a white gown—a dress with fitted lace sleeves, in similar style to his strangely cut jacket, and a skirt so long she would have to be careful not to trip. He even combed her hair back and tapped some color onto her lips with his finger.

When his work was done, the man looked incredibly pleased with the result of his labor. Brenya just felt ridiculous.

A string of glittering stones was set about her throat. When it did not elicit a response, Jacques frowned. "These were my mother's. Before that, my grandmothers. And so on."

She had not asked for them, or for the dress, or the paint on her lips, or the butterflies in her stomach. "I have never worn jewelry before."

He stroked her cheek. "Only Bernard women wear this necklace."

Whatever significance that moment held for him was lost on her, Brenya aware she was doing something wrong. Hand patting the shape of the tangling web, she looked down to see a spangle of light across her breasts. Where the gown was cut low they sat like a beacon, made all the brighter next to her tan skin.

They were pretty. Far too pretty for her.

"I don't fully understand the concept of motherhood or Centrists' focus on lineage. Annette took such joy in holding and feeding her son. Your mother must have been the same way. I don't even know the name of the female who birthed me."

He ran a finger down her jaw, smirking at her statement. "Would you like to know it?"

"No. That knowledge has no value to me. It does not define who I am."

"Some days, I envy you that, *mon chou*." He took the fingers still pressed to his family bauble and drew them to his mouth for a kiss. "There is plenty of time for me to teach you all you need to know. Someday, you too will take joy in holding and feeding our child, but there is no need to rush such things. Under my mother's early advice, I have been taking contraceptives since... adolescence made use of them wise. When you are ready, I'll stop. Until then, we'll enjoy one another."

It was such a strange topic to insert into conversation that Brenya scowled, unsure what to make of it. She had not imagined herself in Annette's position for even a moment, had not considered that someday Jacques might expect her to procreate.

Years ago she had been notified she was not fit for the breeding banks. She had accepted it, relieved, in fact, that nothing would interfere with her duties. In Beta sector, once an idea was set, it was constant. In Central, things did not work that way. Everything shifted, impermanent and enigmatic.

"What troubles you? The thought of children or the thought of no children?"

Neither and both. "I don't know if it's appropriate that I wear your mother's necklace. I am not your mate."

Jade eyes grew dark, Jacques' tone lowering significantly. "You will be."

On that point, she felt there was nothing to add. Smoothing her hands over the flowing skirt he'd chosen for her, Brenya asked, "Is there significance in the color of the dress?"

"You look beautiful in white."

Annette's advice teased her memory, leading

Brenya to offer a compliment in return. "I've never seen you wear your hair loose outside of…"

Smirking like the devil, he finished her sentence, "When we play?"

She could feel a blush creep over her chest and cheeks and could not fathom the why of it. "It looks nice."

HE HAD EXPLAINED to her in detail what to expect. A State dinner was a weekly event, this one particularly important as Bernard Dome had let in its first foreigners since the entry hatch was sealed over a century ago. Ambassador Jules Havel was the guest of honor.

She was not required to talk to him.

Brenya was not required to perform in any way. Annette would see to her entertainment while the Alphas conversed. All she need do was sit by his side and enjoy herself.

Simple enough.

Except Brenya had come to learn that nothing was simple, or straightforward, or honest in this place.

After a walk through halls and rooms Brenya had not ventured through before, the couple in white arrived at a set of double doors. Behind those gilded panels a long table waited, set with linen and more silverware, plates, and crystal glasses than necessary for the amount of guests in attendance.

Alpha males of all adult ages, dressed just as absurdly as the Commodore, talked amongst themselves.

There were no females in attendance... except Annette, who smiled, and, careful of her tender body, made her way over to kiss Brenya on the cheek. "I'm thrilled to be included. I can't tell you how good it is to be allowed out of bed!"

Brenya could not help but agree, her innocent comment drawing the titters of many neighboring men, including a rich laugh from the Alpha at her side.

Instantly embarrassed, she colored.

Jacques pressed his smiling lips to her ear. "Come. You sit here beside me. Drink some wine, it will help you relax."

Everyone followed the Commodore's cue, the rustle of chairs and the economic movement of bodies taking their assigned places short-lived. Annette smiled, nearly across from her, but there were two chairs left unclaimed directly before the Commodore and his 'mate's' position.

One had to be for Ancil, the other for the Ambassador.

Brenya, as usual in this place, was incorrect.

The owners of those honored seats arrived moments later, Annette rising to rush beaming toward the door once Security Advisor Ancil Dubois was announced. The gilded wood opened, and the look on the blonde's face went from ecstatic to heartbroken.

Another female was on her esteemed husband's arm. Another woman had all his attention, Ancil so transfixed he walked right past his wife to announce. "We apologize, Commodore, for our tardiness."

The apology seemed only a formality, Jacques in the exact same languid position as if all were natural and expected—an elbow on his chair's carved armrest, an unharried smile on his lips.

As the couple came forward, so did the scent... an odor Brenya had grown very familiar with in the last weeks.

Alpha, Omega fluids. Sex.

The room was oblivious to Annette's horror, men shouting congratulations, spoons being rung against crystal goblets.

The black-haired woman, beautiful by every possible measure, smiled at the congratulations. Pushing her pin-straight sheet of hair from her shoulder, she revealed where teeth had punctured, the mark still swollen, for all to see.

The cheers grew louder.

When Brenya moved to stand, Jacques put a hand to her thigh. The silent command to remain seated, to leave Annette struck and alone, made the Omega turn her head and glare. "What's going on?"

The Commodore replied, "A cause for celebration. The first pair-bond under Bernard Dome since the time of our great-grandfathers. Ancil has claimed his mate."

"He has a wife." A perfect wife who had just given birth to his son.

"There is more news." Ancil's voice rang out, the man waving an arm to silence the room and declare, "We were blessed in our joining. Lucia is with child."

A small voice behind them muttered, "No…"

It was then Ancil deigned to turn his head so he might look at his wife after her negation of his joy. Brenya could not see his expression, but the anguish on Annette's face mirrored horrific pain.

Tears were falling over pretty cheeks, Annette hardly able to call out to him, "Ancil?"

Ancil's reply was harsh. "Sit."

Stumbling toward the table, Annette obeyed, her body moving as if pulled along by marionette strings.

It was a show for the room, a vast table of

Alphas watching with rapt attention as Ancil brought his wife to heel. The blonde was placed at his left, the dark-haired Omega at his right, and in the middle Ancil sat nodding greetings to the nearest male. "Ambassador."

"This is wrong." Silence descended across the room at Brenya's proclamation. Chest rising and falling, she looked from Annette, to her husband, to the unknown woman who dared to glare back at her. "You have a wife."

"And by our marriage contract, signed by said Beta wife, I am also allowed to take a mate should the opportunity arise. All is legal and will stand in court if questioned." Ancil lowered his chin, dark eyes hostile. "Ask your Commodore if you doubt my claims."

Brenya could not stop her tongue or the thundering of her heart. "When Annette signed it, there were no Omegas in Bernard Dome."

"Yet she signed the standard contract all the same."

"Standard?" Every marriage in Central followed such twisted rules? Were all Alphas just biding their time?

It was Annette, her eyes downcast to the table before her who whispered, "Brenya, please be quiet."

Swallowing, Brenya thought she might be sick.

Her eyes went around the table, to the men gawking... all the strangers... and it was she they found fault with, not Ancil and his Omega.

Under the table, Jacques squeezed her thigh, but made no move to alter his bored expression or say a word on the subject. The only thing he did say was, "Please serve," to the waiting staff.

A team of synchronized Betas poured wine, removing the golden cloche before each guest so the first course might be enjoyed.

It did not look like any kind of food Brenya was accustomed to. It was just one small egg, smeared with sauce atop a lettuce leaf. She hardly noticed it once something much more appetizing twinged her nostrils and caused her head to snap up.

Not every member of the party had been served the same plate.

There was a bowl in front of Annette. Inside the china dish something Brenya had asked for and been denied.

Beta rations—the pharmaceutically laced food that turned a person into a cog. Food that would deaden Annette's emotions and make her a drone just like Brenya had been.

When the blonde began to understand what waited before her, her silent tears turned to sobs. And still... still she picked up her spoon.

"Don't eat it!" Brenya was half out of her chair,

struggling against the weight of Jacques' grip on her leg. Reaching across the table, she fought and failed to slap the food from Annette's hands. "Annette, no. Don't eat it!"

The golden spoon was shaking before Annette's parted lips, Ancil turning to snarl at his wife.

The low threat of his growl was enough to push the woman over the edge. She shoved the poisoned food in her mouth, weeping as she swallowed.

Frantic, Brenya called out, "Stop!"

"Annette, it seems your presence is disruptive. Leave the table. The remainder of your meal will be taken in your room." Ancil waved over a servant, ordering him to gather both the food and his wife at once.

Orders were obeyed without question. The door opened, Annette rounded away, and when the portal closed, something in Brenya snapped.

Ancil smirked at her look of hatred. "From now on, Lucia will serve as your companion. Annette will be busy raising my children and have no time for you."

Silence cut at her skin, fueling the fire growing behind her eyes.

Staring down a horrible man, a voice came from Brenya as if born from another person. "As a Beta I labored every day to assure your safety, took on the most dangerous assignments, conducted complex repairs so you would survive. I studied harder, worked longer than any of my peers. I pushed the limits of my mind and body more times than I can remember. Tirelessly, each morning I spoke the same oath everyone under this Dome is trained to recite.

"It is my sworn duty to protect the Dome and all who live within.

"I meant those words. I love and would die for the people of Bernard Dome without question. There was cohesion and flawless symmetry amongst my peers. We did not compete or compare.

"And then I was brought here and I met you. I was told I could not be a Beta anymore, that my training, education, and expertise were no longer necessary. My entire purpose for existing is a joke to you, *the Commodore's disfigured Omega toy*.

"Now I am learning the ways of Central. There is no oath recited upon waking here. You serve yourselves and scheme. You abuse your females. You eat off china plates and drink wine from five different crystal glasses. You're cruel, and you are selfish.

"If life in Central is a reflection of humanity before the Red Consumption, I can clearly see why everybody died. I now understand why Domes have failed. It was not due to women like me. It was due to men like you.

"You are a disease.

"But ultimately you are powerless. Should catastrophe strike, who would you come running to? You would come running to me. Would I help you? I don't know anymore. I dislike you more than any person I have met in my life."

A snide lip curled, Ancil absently swishing wine in his goblet. "Control your female, Jacques. I don't believe she's learned her place."

Brenya was far from done. "I will find a way to make you pay for what you've done to Annette."

Fingers came around her throat, and they were not Ancil's. Jacques held her in mirror to how he enjoyed restraining her when fucking her face on. Only he was not staring at her in wonderment, but in rage. No words were spoken as he forced her body back, as he squeezed to the point she gasped.

Bracing for the coming blow, instead Brenya found herself dragged from table, feet catching on the carpet and tangling in her long skirt.

He'd dragged her somewhere this way once before, and she was soon to learn the outcome would be the same.

His words were colder than the diamonds cutting into her throat. "Pardon me, gentlemen, lady. I need to have a word with my mate."

The door closed, Brenya unsure what room they were in. There was no time to look before he bent her over the back of a couch. It was a marvel how quickly he bunched up her skirt, how violently he tore away the thin scrap of silk covering her sex. She could hardly reach back and try to stop him before he made the noise that would slicken her passage. Then his cock shoved in, Jacques fucking her so hard the couch scratched over the floor with each thrust.

"You are never to threaten an Alpha! You are never to put yourself in danger that way!"

Ribs pressed into the sculpted wooden top of the sofa, Brenya could not breathe to reply. She could do nothing but kick her leg in an attempt to brace.

His invasion was all she knew, every stretch and pull of her cunt distracting until she was caught up and drowning past her horror and grief.

He'd promised he'd never strike her in anger. This was so much worse.

"You are never to growl at a male!"

Had she done that to Ancil, or had she done it to Jacques when he'd taken her throat in his fist? Was she growling at him now? She could not think, could do nothing but claw at the couch.

"There are laws, Brenya, and he broke none. Do not presume to know better than your leadership. Do not presume to think you know what is best for

Annette. Would you have her languish away the rest of her days watching her husband adore another? He has shown her a mercy in this."

If it was possible for the Alpha to grow rougher, he did. Rapid jerks of his hips punished her from behind. It was domination, pure and simple, and she could do nothing.

Meaner still, he reached under her body and began to patiently circle her clit.

Brenya found that, in fact, she was capable of making a noise. A single cry, the single chirp of a dying bird.

He compelled her climax and knotted her right there in the antechamber of the dining hall where servants might walk by with trays of food.

Everything, every grunt, every shout—every last thing he'd done had been heard by those inside.

When he began to spurt, the male changed tactics to draw out the pleasure he'd forced on her.

Face twisted up, eyes scrunched close, Brenya tried to shut it out, but she was full of him, unable to escape. In the blink of an eye, he became another person entirely, cooing at her, petting her back, soothing her buttocks with a kneading grip.

Strong arms came around her sore middle, Jacques gathering her back, pulling her until he'd found a seat and could settle her, joined as they were, facing forward on his lap. At her ear he whispered, "Now calm yourself, *mon chou*. We will take this time to gather our thoughts before we return to our friends."

He was still pulsating in her belly, and she had yet to come down from the high. Should she catch her reflection, her pupils would be blown, her eyes almost completely black.

As black as the Commodore's heart. As black as her hate for Ancil.

Brenya refused to speak, no matter how Jacques cooed of her beauty, how much he claimed to adore her, how it was his duty to keep her safe... even from herself. Staring forward, she felt his hands caress where they would, felt the soft kisses on her neck and under her ear, and fantasized about deconstructing the air filtration in Ancil's room. It would take her less than five minutes to alter the mechanism so it pumped carbon dioxide over the sleeping Alpha.

He would die weak and gasping.

When the knot began to subside, Jacques reached for a swath of lace laying over the polished mahogany table at his elbow. He brought it between her spread legs, using that delicate thing to mop up the rush of fluid at his retreat, dabbing at her sore labia before tossing it aside as if it were disposable.

Exactly how Ancil had tossed Annette away.

Jacques drew her to stand, bending down to right her skirts and make sure all signs of their coupling were covered. Yet she reeked of him, of Alpha musk, and of her failures. Her torn undergarments were gathered from the floor and stuffed in his pocket.

When Jacques took her face in his hands and turned it to look down upon her, her eyes spurned his.

He spoke anyway. "I accept that you will most likely refuse to speak to me for the remainder of the evening. But we *will* speak on this later. You think to play at games you do not understand, and must learn such things can be deadly." He dared to press a lingering kiss to her slack lips. "I know you're angry, but you took your punishment well. I suggest you do not put me in the position of having to do it again."

Taking her elbow, he led her back into the dining hall, pulled out her chair before all the staring faces, and sat her down. They had missed a course, and she had yet to eat, but when the soup arrived Brenya continued to stare forward at nothing, prompting Jacques to lean over and warn her. "Eat."

It was mechanical, spoon to mouth, tasteless cold green sludge sliding down her throat. Several more courses arrived, talk around the table having picked up as if nothing had happened. If Ancil was staring at her and gloating, she did not see. If he was fawning over his new, pregnant mate, she never knew. Her eyes were boring a hole into the wall.

It was the only way to keep from breaking things.

16

W hen dinner ended, there was still more entertainment to be had— more *guests* set to join the festivities. Jacques stood to announce, "In the adjacent room companions of the female and Omega variety await our attention," to the raucous applause of the room.

The Commodore grinned, offering his hand to the brooding Omega so they might make their way into the adjacent chamber. "Your place is at my side, Brenya."

Her place.

Looking at his outstretched palm, did not move her to take it. She could not bring herself to raise her fingers and obey. It was not an act of rebellion; it was the effect of finally comprehending that she was more a slave than even what Ancil intended to fashion Annette into.

Because she could feel, and it was awful.

Jacques wanted to take her to the room he'd punished her in. In that room that smelled of her slick, his come, and the lingering cloud of aggression and anger, she was to stand by his side and submit.

"I can't move." Her words were small, a speck of dust in the air.

He took mercy on her, reaching for her elbow to help her stand. When the female was on her feet, he swiped her nearest untouched glass, and held the dessert course's sweet white wine to her lips. "Drink. It will help."

Gulping gracelessly, she swallowed every last drop. She even stood still as Jacques leaned down to kiss a renegade dribble from her chin, her disgust only betrayed by the closing of her eyes and rapid rate of her breath when he drew near.

"I didn't hurt you, *mon chou*. Your reaction is a bit extreme. Don't you think?"

She could not dissect the tone of the lips at her ear—if he was warning her, if he was offering comfort, she could not tell. All she could do was dip her chin and hope he'd leave her be.

"Why do I get the sense that your nod is the first time you've lied to me?" Impatience made his voice far less beautiful. "Open your eyes. Look at me and tell me why you're shaking."

Lashes parted, Brenya vaguely aware that the other males had already gone ahead. She looked into eyes the color of envy and muttered the honest truth in her heart. "You're a monster."

A long, agitated sigh came from the Alpha. Eyeing her, he offered a condescending bow. "Truer words have never been spoken."

And then he left her there, rejoining his guests with a smile painted on his face as if he were king of the world.

Brenya supposed he was.

Unsure what to do with herself, she wandered as far from the party as the dining room would allow. Positioned beside a grand window overlooking the architectural splendor of Central, she looked down at the city she had dedicated her life to, and did not recognize it at all.

"Those are the Bernard family diamonds. I have not seen them grace the neck of a woman since Jacques' mother wore them." It was meant to be a compliment, Brenya could tell by the kind tone of the elderly Alpha who'd approached. That did not mean it was welcome.

Exhausted, she spoke to the view. "He said as much."

Rheumy eyes looked over her profile, lingering

on her scar. "He never dressed his tarts in something of such value, dear girl. The statement in having you wear them now is… interesting. Just what do you suppose he is trying to say?"

Turning her back to the window, arms limp at her side, Brenya found more than the old Alpha had crossed the room to speak with her. Beside him stood an unsmiling Beta. There was a lifelessness in the stranger's expression that mirrored exactly the way she wished she felt.

Empty instead of wretched.

"You must be Ambassador Jules Havel."

"I am."

She had no idea what to say to him, no idea what she was doing. "Did you enjoy your dinner?"

He blinked, abrupt in his answer. "No."

Whatever they wanted, whatever reason they had for breaking from the party and coming to her, Brenya didn't care. All she desired was to be left alone. "Neither did I."

The old man had more to say. "It would be unwise for you to remain in here by yourself. You have not been bonded yet and the men are drinking and enamored with their company. They are distracted."

Distracted? Stealing a glance in the direction of the open doors, Brenya found several of the available Omegas lingering near Jacques, laughing as he spoke. One was even touching his arm. She was a beauty on rival with Annette: icy hair, flawless skin, eyes as blue and clear as the sky.

Standing side by side they were a matched set. How many weeks before that lovely Omega was wearing the diamonds?

Inevitability stared her in the face. "You're right. I should leave."

It seemed rude to say such a thing before the Ambassador, but the old man did not hesitate. "You're missing my point, Miss Brenya Perin. Those Omegas did not come all this way to be mated to mid-level bureaucrats. Go in there and remind them who is wearing the Bernard jewels."

Her time in Central had taught her one thing, the old man would not be making such a suggestion unless the potential action benefited him in some way. In what way, she could not say. She didn't comprehend any of the plots and schemes everyone here lived and breathed.

Her attention went back to the Beta, the limpid blue of his eyes a bit jarring. Her motivation for attempted polite conversation was halted by that look, and she was relieved that they might stand still and be silent.

Until he ruined it by speaking in an accent as ugly as hers. "You should leave."

Heart heavy, she turned back to the view and sighed. "I don't know how to get out."

"Brenya!" Jacques called, the sound of his footsteps crossing the room like soft thunder. "Come."

He was smiling when she glanced his way, but his eyes were malicious as he looked upon the men standing near her.

Once upon their group, the Commodore immediately put an arm around Brenya's waist and pulled her flush to his side. "Come away from them now and return to your monster. I find myself greedy for your attention."

He was purring loudly, so loud it seemed almost inappropriate. The sound coupled with the wine in her veins led her to beg, "Please, Jacques, I'd like to go to bed."

Twisting her words with a devilish smirk, Jacques teased. "I'd be a fool to resist such an offer."

The old man dared to laugh. The Ambassador did not.

HE CARRIED her from the party in his arms, despite her yelp when he'd gone to swoop her up. On one hand, she'd hated it, embarrassed he made such a show of their departure for the group to chuckle at.

On the other, it had given her a way to avoid conversation or contact with anyone else. Fingers toying with the lapel of his jacket, she'd kept her eyes on Jacques' chest and off the room where he'd shamed her over the back of a couch.

She'd even held her breath so she would not have to smell a thing.

When they were in the halls, she closed her eyes and settled against his body, certain asking him to put her down would have been pointless.

Jacques kept his silence all the way to his rooms. When they were at the bed, he lay her down with a grin.

"My poor Omega. She had a terrible night and hates me." Jacques took off her shoes and kissed the tip of her toes, kneading Brenya's feet as he teased, "What would make her feel better?"

Brenya reached for one of the larger pillows, her favorite one, and pulled it to her body as if she might curl around it and forget. "You said I didn't have to talk to you."

He nipped her toe, earning a squeal, before lowering himself over her body. "I know what you'd like."

She wanted out of the constrictive dress. She wanted the jagged necklace off her skin. But to say so would be used as an excuse by the male to have his way with her.

Which he was going to do either way.

It was more than the weight of the Alpha hovering over her, a heavy burden sat on her chest. Eyes closed tight, she sighed into the pillow. "I'd like Annette to be happy."

"And she will be." He was playful for a monster, kissing and biting his way up her body. "It is my duty to see that all under the Dome have purpose. Annette will find hers in raising Ancil's children. She will find it in service as a Beta beyond the title of first wife."

"You mean Lucia's children."

"The eldest and heir is hers. The law is clear on that, Lucia's progeny will always be second. It will be the same for the other wives when they too are replaced. The contracted lineage is protected in case a mate is found after marriage."

"You have reduced her to something disposable." Trying to turn under him and give him her back, Brenya grumbled, "And the other wives, will they be made into mindless servants? Will they be discarded and abused?"

"That is up to their husbands." Jacques grumbled at her lack of response to his games, turning her body where he would. Like a child denied a toy he barked, "I do not like you sullen, *mon chou*. Loving me can be very easy."

Mumbling into the pillow, Brenya rejected the

idea. "No."

"What did you say to me?"

Eyes open, emboldened by how much anger was in her heart, Brenya turned to face him so he might hear clearly. "I said no."

The immediate stink of Alpha anger singed her nostrils, Jacques glaring down, his lips tight and eyes hard. Long moments passed while he studied her face, the sounds of the bones in his fingers popping when he made a fist.

It looked as if his every muscle swelled. "You are not the only Omega in Bernard Dome, Brenya."

And there were nine unmated, beautiful women ready to laugh and play his games. "I've seen what you do to women who are inconvenient, what you did to your friend—the public shaming. The display. First Annette, then me. I do not doubt you will do it to the other Omegas too."

He went from fuming to furious. "You know I can make you like anything I choose to do to you. I can make you cry out for me on my whim. I own this body of yours, heart and soul. You're mine no matter your refusal or tonight's paltry rebellion. I can do things to you in the dark that, come morning, will leave you smiling and humming in my arms."

He was going to hurt her for saying what she would, might even have her terminated that night. It didn't matter; resentment had control of her tongue.

"Like bend me over a couch and rape me while your awful friends listen?"

"You came. There was no blood, I checked." He reared back to his knees, large and looming, every vein in his neck standing out as he growled, "More importantly, ignorant Omega, the lesson was one you should take to heart. I'd rather abuse you, as you put it, than give any of those males cause to see to your demise. Every player at court is dangerous. If I don't correct you, they will. If I fail to mark you as mine, one of them will take you. Ancil was the greatest contender, now he has his own mate to protect. I may no longer have to worry about him salivating over you, but he is the last Alpha under the Dome you want as an enemy."

His explanation did nothing to cool her temper, in fact, it drove her to grind her teeth. "I didn't say abused, I said raped."

Jacques slammed a fist into the mattress, snarling, "I demand you forgive me this instant!"

"NO!"

There was a deafening roar of a monster pushed too far.

Self-preservation broke through Brenya's rage. She stilled, watching the threat stare down at her as if ready to snap her neck.

When the man grew instantly, unnervingly composed, when he smiled as if formulating something truly terrible, she was already shaking her head no and trying to scramble away.

"Brenya…" In a flash he had her wrists in a careful grasp, rubbing his thumbs in soft circles over vulnerable flesh. "Brenya, where are you going?"

Refusing to answer, she faced the predator and lay as still as stone.

He set one of her hands free, collecting the fingers of the other to rub one by one. Next he turned her palm upward, his thumbs kneading the flesh. Her wrist, forearm, elbow all received attention. When his grip made it to her shoulder, Brenya swallowed, sure her neck was next.

Would he look her in the eye as he broke it? Or would it be a slow strangulation?

Menacing fingertips trailed over diamond covered collarbones, moving to the opposite shoulder. He treated the second arm as the first, gently working stiff muscle groups, holding her gaze with misleading, soft eyes.

Warm palms engulfed her rib cage, smoothing downward over flank and hip. Over her skirt he kneaded a thigh, taking ages to feel out all tension and reflexively command it away. The lightest of purrs colored the air, the male inhaling deep and slow as he watched her, until Brenya too was mirroring his breath.

Over many long minutes, antagonism drained

into the mattress, the hypnotic power of his purr, the slow moving touch of his hands instilling an inescapable physical response. Her eyes grew heavy, so heavy she could hardly keep them open. She was already fading into dreamland when he slowly turned her body over.

The soft grate of the zipper was ignored under the weight of his purr. She even groaned into the pillow when those warm hands began to work on her uncovered back.

It was many hours before she woke to find herself naked, tucked into bed, the Bernard diamonds still strung around her throat. There was no Alpha body warming hers. But he was there, watching her from his chair, Jacques' jade eyes aglow in the dark.

17

Greth Dome

He had promised her a new world, but standing in it felt strange. Where Thólos, in its glory, had been cramped concrete and crowds, there was little of that in her life anymore. Greth was built to mirror nature, rocks, growing things, water—all amidst civilization.

But she avoided Followers. She avoided the city below.

Though Shepherd had not voiced it, Claire knew he would rather keep her separate from his men— too many Alphas coming and going. Twice she had tried to walk outside her rooms, to see if she could do it. The first time she had hardly crossed the threshold, unable to move further. The second time she walked to the palace grounds. Shepherd had been at a distance, working with his men. He was her goal, her first test of herself in ages.

Those silver eyes had watched her every step, her mate having been notified of her approach. When he'd gone still, so had the rest of them—as if they were all infected somehow by her being there. Those first steps ended right past the carved wood doors that separated living quarters from bureaucracy. Claire had frozen, actually immobile, and could not move forward or back. There was some weird limbo, a feeling of wobbling in her belly.

It had been a beautiful day, one of the first in spring. It had also been the second day since she had secretly stopped taking all her medication.

Anxiety was an old ghost, but in those moments —on that first solid try—the ghost had become the devil himself, and Claire could hardly hear over the sound of blood rushing in her ears. Unsure of the expression on her face, all she could think was that it had to be bad for Shepherd to have made his way to her so quickly.

"Have you come here to see me, little one? There was no need for you to leave the nest to do so. I could have been contacted." Shepherd's large hand closed over her shoulder, the man frowning because she had unknowingly wandered out in only her nightclothes and robe. "I will return you to our home."

"I don't want to go there." But he was already herding her away from the inner workings of his order, shuffling her toward a high walled segment of the palace grounds very few would dare to enter.

"Why? Are you displeased with our home?"

Swallowing, Claire felt her legs move because he moved her. "No, Shepherd. It is a beautiful home." And it was; it was lovely.

"Then why would you come here, little one? Are you lonely, do you require companionship?"

No, she did not want companions. "I don't need a babysitter, Shepherd. I just wanted to take a walk."

He stopped, his highly polished shoes suddenly silent, and Shepherd looked down at the woman held pressed to his side. She hadn't been sleeping and it showed in the dark smears under her eyes. "A walk that has left you badly panicked, Claire."

She was so tempted to bury her nose in his side and let him make her feel better. "I want to be like I was before. I want to feel normal again."

It was almost cruel the way he said, "You are never going to feel the way you did before. You are never going to be who you were before."

He could feel the tumult of emotions raging

inside her, the fear growing weaker in place of despair, anger, hate, pain, but most of all love. Everything that could be done to fix what hurt her, he was doing. Even her current state he could improve, and did when he pulled off his jacket and set it over her shoulders so she might not feel undressed before his men.

That old challenging look in her green eyes reared its head, even though she pulled the warm fabric he'd offered closer. "Thank you."

"CLAIRE HAS BEEN WEANING herself off her medication. Three days ago she stopped taking them all together."

"Such a thing is dangerous! Why was I not informed of this?" Shepherd slammed a fist on the table between them.

Dr. Osin remained at attention, facing her enraged commanding officer, unflinching. "I monitor her closely. This minor rebellion is good for her. She is trying to regain a modicum of control in her life."

"Yet now she hardly sleeps, has an aversion to food. Moreover, it is your job to make her know she can come to me and feel no need for subversion. This *exacerbates* what troubles her."

The older woman had been with the Followers from five years before Thólos fell. Shepherd's rage did not shake dedication like hers. "The side-effects will pass. But you disrupted her progress by ushering her away the moment she grew scared. Claire was in no danger and needs to learn the proper time and place for fear without the crutch of sedation. Next time, if she pushes her boundaries and requires comfort, you wait for her to walk to you. Secondly, confronting her about the medication would be unwise. Say nothing. Build trust."

Shepherd had a great dislike for the old woman these days. "Should you be wrong and she grows unhappy, I will kill you and replace you. It will not be an easy death."

The threat did not unsettle one grey hair on Dr. Osin's head.

Maybe there was a silver lining. Angry, yet hopefully, Shepherd asked, "Has she also ceased taking her heat suppressant?"

"No, sir. Those are diligently swallowed morning and night."

How he hated those little blue pills.

Shepherd left the psychiatrist and entered the enclosure around the home he'd had built for his mate. Claire was in her garden, ripping at plants, painfully unskilled in their keeping. Before he could even address her, she glared over her shoulder and snapped, "I'm not taking all those drugs anymore, all right. I *will* feel normal again. I want to be able to focus and carry on a conversation without getting confused. When you tell me you love me, I want to be able to feel it!"

Her unsolicited honesty kept him silent. Shepherd took a seat on the nearby bench and nodded. She was so angry with him. It came over her some days and burned Shepherd on his end of the link, but she had never once vocalized her feelings. She didn't have to. He could read her like a book. Antidepressants, antipsychotics, sedatives kept that feeling blurred under medicinal apathy, but it blazed with no chemicals flowing through her bloodstream. And with her fury was twice as much guilt.

But the guilt was his. "Everything was my fault."

Her trowel jammed into the earth, Claire oddly comforted that he knew her insides were a mess. She did not speak of Thólos, not with him, not with Dr. Osin. Any reminder set her off. "You were right. I can't be who I was."

"You can be something else."

She was only one thing now. "I suppose I am. I am your wife now."

The modest band was dirty from her work in her garden, but Shepherd's eyes found pleasure in seeing it on her finger because the title was one that mattered to her. She'd mentioned many times in the past, her dream of her future *husband*, so he'd spoken her culture's vows to please her. "You are, little one: my wife and mate. You are also a sub-par gardener."

Claire laughed, her eyes glittering as the rage dwindled and amusement seeped in. "Maybe I'd be a better soldier."

"You would not."

His teasing made her laugh again. When the sound faded, her mercurial emotions found momentary neutrality. "I'm going to go running on the causeway over the city where we walk."

"I will accompany you."

"I don't want you to. I want to run by myself."

It was very difficult for Shepherd to remain silent and trust Dr. Osin's advice. "Do not forget to wear a windbreaker. It can grow very cold near the updrafts."

An hour later, Claire sprinted down the vacant path until her body shook from exertion, and she'd loved every minute of it. She'd panted heavily and bent over, near vomiting. She did the same the next day, then the next. She ran as fast as she could, darting through shrubbery, jumping over stairs. She ran until it hurt.

That distracting pain was preferable to the ache she couldn't shake.

Shepherd had her shadowed each time, attempting more than once to do so himself, but Claire was too fast. So when reports came back, weeks later, of how she'd stopped in her run—how she'd sobbed, her hand pressed over her womb— he'd just about strangled Dr. Osin, but released the old woman's throat before more than bruises would result.

Claire had returned home, oblivious. She'd prepared dinner for them. She'd smiled and been happy. And then she'd reached for his belt buckle and gone to her knees.

18

"What did it feel like the first time you saw him?"

Another aggravating morning with Dr. Osin. They had been doing this for too long, going through the motions, wasting one another's time. "The snow... he was hard to see. I *felt* him, heard him calling. Shepherd was smiling."

There was a pause. "So you jumped from the causeway to reach him?"

"You already know I did."

"I do. Which is why I asked you what you felt the *first* time you saw Shepherd."

There was a twitch Claire could not suppress, a tightening around her mouth. "I was cold."

"You were frightened?"

Claire could hardly put voice behind her answer. "Yes."

"Tell me why."

And this is where the session would dead-end. Claire was stubborn, and Thólos was a time she would not think of. "Why do you think?"

The old woman spoke directly. "He is dangerous. Larger than you. Violent. Intelligent."

Claire could not help but agree. "He didn't look at me when I asked for a moment of his time."

"Did he hurt you?"

"No. He saved me..." Claire shook her head and amended, "I thought he saved me. He used me."

"In estrous?"

"I *hate* estrous." All of them had been disastrous, terrifying, or a weakness she could not defend herself from.

The woman adjusted her glasses and looked up from her notes. "I am an Alpha, my deceased mate Omega. Estrous is a thing we experienced roughly three times a year. It was celebrated."

What did that matter? "You're a female Alpha. It's different."

"He feared estrous initially too. Male Omegas are one in a million. I found him on the poorest levels. I took him."

Claire sneered. "You're a bitch."

"He did love to call me that. He also loved me, greatly."

Green eyes moved from the wall she chose to stare at during these talks to fix directly on her psychiatrist. "And still he died."

"Of cancer, twelve years ago."

"I'm sorry." She hadn't meant to say something so cruel, aware the monotone of her doctor must hide great pain. "I am sorry."

"You love him."

There was no need for Claire to confirm. "I know he makes you come here, that you had a position far more interesting than dealing with me. For that I am sorry, but I don't want to talk to you."

Dr. Osin's voice was smooth, focused. "My job remains the same. All Followers are analyzed by me. In this new world, I decide who is fit to serve our cause and who must be removed." There was no pride behind the doctor's next statement. "When it comes to psychology I am the best in Shepherd's army, subsequently the best in the world."

And almost as arrogant as Shepherd himself. "Then you must resent this new assignment."

A pencil went back to the pad on the doctor's knee. "That would be petty."

Speaking so their meeting might end, Claire said, "I like running over the city. We could talk about that."

"Well, Claire, thank you for throwing me a bone. But no. Let's talk about Shepherd."

Claire mimicked the annoying woman's monotone. "We were married twelve weeks ago. He gave me an emerald I could barter for a small country, which I never wear. So he had a band made for me. He wore black slacks and a formal jacket. I wore a green dress I had never seen before and did not choose. He likes to pick my clothes. I have no idea where they come from. We took our vows outside, by that little fountain near the trees."

"Were you happy?"

It was the first time positive emotion came into Claire's voice at one of her appointments. "Very happy."

"What did you think of Shepherd the first time you saw him in Thólos?"

Those good feelings were swept from under Claire's feet. "He scared me."

"Elaborate, Claire."

Claire snapped. "Everyone I knew was dead or dying. *Everyone.* The streets were a nightmare. Omegas were being ripped in half, slaughtered. Every day we lost more. All my friends… gone. There was no haven, not even when I went to Shepherd."

"He gave you sanctuary."

"But the Omegas…"

The old woman knew just how to gain a reaction. "You went to save them. They betrayed you."

Claire started shouting, standing from her chair as she paced, "They were starving! Their children and mates murdered before their eyes!"

"And you lost a child."

Instantly deflated, Claire shrank. "No. No, no, no."

"You lost your son."

"Be quiet!"

"You named him Collin. You were hurt so badly you miscarried."

Claire could hardly believe it. "Hurt?"

The doctor adjusted her glasses. "What would you call it?"

She was so fucking tired of the grind. "You know what happened. There is no reason for this!"

"What happened in Thólos, Claire?"

"Shepherd released a nightmare, and they did to me the same thing they did to everyone else."

"What did they do to you?"

She could not say the word, even knowing that was the key to silencing the constant preaching from the old woman. "They died that day. They can't do it again."

Dr. Osin looked up from her notes. "Though they were wounded, not all of them died when

Premier Dane found you. Some crawled away in the rush."

Claire began to shake. "What?"

"Shepherd found where the rats hid in the Undercroft the night he brought you home. Now they are dead, and died painfully."

Those men had deserved to die. Knowing her mate had done horrible things to them should have angered her, upset her morals. It didn't. It only made her feel better. "I'm glad."

"Are you?"

There was no need to hesitate in answering. "Yes."

"Why?"

There was no rehabilitation for that kind of evil. "I'll sleep better at night knowing they'll never hurt anyone else."

"How did they hurt you?"

There was some bubbling horror spewing out her mouth she couldn't stop. A terrible name. "Svana... three convicts."

Dr. Osin watched Claire begin to panic, nodding at her to continue.

Claire could hardly choke the words out. "They made a game of it."

"Define *it*. What happened to you, Claire?"

What happened in Thólos? WHAT HAPPENED IN THÓLOS? Every fucking day she tried to forget, needed *not* to remember, but the bitch doctor wouldn't leave her alone. Shepherd wouldn't leave her alone. Enough was enough. Claire kicked at the coffee table between them, wood hitting the old woman's shins. Flying from the room, Claire ran so hard it hurt, ran to accuse the one who thought this torment would help her.

He needed to see what he'd done. Shepherd needed to pay! There was no pause at the gates of the palace, no shrinking back from the nearness of strangers.

Angry, *furious*, she bounded toward Shepherd and started screaming, "They raped me, Shepherd! Is that what you want to hear so fucking badly? Is that why I have to sit with that horrible woman every day? RAPED! Over and over, in every way, until our baby died, and then they raped me some more! THAT'S WHAT FUCKING HAPPENED IN THÓLOS!"

Dr. Osin had run up behind her, the sound of the woman's footsteps the only noise in the courtyard. Soldiers seemed stuck where they were, frozen in that horrible moment of time. Even Shepherd.

It seemed to hit Claire, where she was and how she got there. Streams already ran down her cheeks. She was red, heart racing, and the feeling of anguish grew. Sobs started, managing breath was difficult, and then Shepherd was there, giving her a place to hide her face against his chest.

Fingers carded through dark hair, Shepherd doing his best to keep his voice even. "You will tell me everything that happened, and I will listen. You can scream it if you need to."

She was shaking her head even as she whimpered, "My hands were tied above my head. I was naked on a dirty mattress deep underground. Svana fingered me, said she wished she could stay and watch... I told her I loved you. She laughed."

The fingers in her hair seemed to catch, become claws, but Shepherd continued petting her as best he could.

"There were three Alphas. They were filthy and smiling. I couldn't feel much the first time from the drugs *you'd* forced on me. I just laid there and pretended I was somewhere else. They didn't like that." The story continued in graphic detail, Shepherd holding her tight as the room cleared. Claire told him every last detail she could remember, even some she had forgotten, they'd been buried so deep. By the end of it, the sobbing had stopped, her voice was detached, her end of the link settled and pained.

"You did well," Shepherd said. "Recounting the trauma is vital to your recovery, little one. It will get easier each time you do it, and you will be less afraid."

Eyes vacant, Claire looked up. "Dr. Osin told me you killed them…"

Shepherd nodded slowly, not at all remorseful.

"Is there proof? I need to see what you did. I need to see them dead."

"No."

"I *need* to see it, Shepherd."

"No," he said softer, pleased Claire's bossiness was rearing its head. "Tomorrow you will recount this to me again. That will do you far more good than looking at horrors."

"Did they suffer?"

"Much more than you did."

Claire was not sure how she felt about that, or why deep down she wished she'd been there to see it. "I don't think I'm a good person anymore."

Arms tightened in their embrace. "You are good, Claire. You're perfect. You're just a little lost right now."

19

Bernard Dome

"Satellite uplink complete. Cue image transfer."

Jacques did not wear his customary impudent smirk. Not for this meeting. He knew enough about who he was dealing with to offer no expression. Every tick and mannerism on either side would be evaluated; every last word would be broken down and reconstructed in search of hidden meanings.

He had accepted the Greth trade agreement. He had accepted the Greth Ambassador. And now it was time for the formal meeting between the Greth and Bernard Dome leaders.

On the wall before them, in a secure room populated by the highest ranking individuals, appeared the massive image of a cold-blooded killer. Like the Beta Ambassador standing at Jacques' side, slithers of black teased out from the collar of the large male's shirt, marking a thick neck almost to jaw. The Alpha's hair was a shade of brown, close cropped in military style, a scar slashed across his lips.

Like Jacques, Shepherd was entirely unsmiling. Like Jacques, he was formally dressed, though it was much easier to imagine the Alpha in fatigues, smeared with blood and sweat.

The images Ancil had uncovered of the man were often times much worse.

"Greetings, Chancellor O'Donnell." Jacques gestured to the Beta Ambassador at his side. "Per your request, Ambassador Havel is present."

"Jules."

The Beta responded at once. "Sir."

When no formal greeting was offered in reply, Jacques continued as if the faux pas were nothing. "Will Queen Svana not be joining us today?"

"My mate is grieving the death of our unborn son. All state matters have been left to my care until she recovers." Shepherd's candor, it would seem, was even more abrupt than his dispassionate Ambassador.

Jacques offered a sympathetic bow. "I offer you both my condolences."

"Your condolences are unnecessary, Jacques Bernard." The Chancellor eyed the Commodore of Bernard Dome, weighing him before cutting his grey eyed gaze to Ambassador Havel. Without preamble, Shepherd began grunting out a language translation programs could not decipher.

Whatever was said, Ambassador Havel responded in equal measure, the pair carrying on a clandestine conversation right before the provoked Bernard Head of State.

Mouth growing tight, open vexation storming into a vicious glance, the Commodore cut off further private conversation. "If you have taken the time to learn French, then speak it." He switched languages, fluidly. "Or do you prefer the Spanish of Greth?" The Commodore's voice modulated again. "Or the English of Thólos?"

"We will speak on Thólos in a moment." There was a twitch at the corner of Shepherd's lips, the nearest thing the psychopath might ever offer to an arrogant smile. "But first, I would like to congratulate you on your upcoming pair-bond. Jules tells me you found a solitary Omega amidst your population and prefer her over those we've offered."

Holding the eye of a male who'd dare condescend, Jacques offered a cold response. "The Omegas offered in trade are lovely. Lucia has already been bonded to my Security Advisor and is with child."

The mention of a child after having admitted the loss of his own changed nothing in Shepherd's demeanor. The male was unflappable. Jacques would remember that. He would remember to keep his own temper in check... especially when the Chancellor was testing how far he might exploit it.

"Trade, it would seem, suits both our cities. When are my orange trees to be prepared for delivery?"

"My master gardeners assure me in three weeks' time the roots will be ready to be packaged for replanting. For your patience, every tree should bloom their first year in Greth."

At last. The news seemed to soften the male filling up the wall. "If they bloom as you say, I will reward you with more Omegas in our spring."

It was as Ambassador Havel had said. The only thing Shepherd was interested in was pleasing his mate. From Jacques' perspective, it seemed the rest of the world could burn for all he cared. "The queen must enjoy oranges very much."

Darkness once again descended upon the Alpha on the screen, a bone-chilling finality in all he said.

"There are no orange trees in Greth Dome, Commodore. The trees she loved were in Thólos, and as your intel must suggest, I destroyed that city. The trees are all dead, the people rot. It is a graveyard."

Cocking a brow, Jacques simpered, the upper hand finally his. "Ten trees for ten fertile Omegas? An offer beyond believing... unless it was never the trees you desired."

"My mate will enjoy your trees, and that will please me. But, no." Shepherd leaned closer as if ready to reach through the screen. "What I desire is... assurances. Therefore, Jules will tell you exactly how and why I destroyed Thólos. I want you to see what the Red Consumption really looks like. And I want you to know that I'm watching. Bernard Dome controls the satellite systems and all external Dome communications. Greth controls a fleet of ships—ships that even now circle the globe intercepting said communications."

Violent eyes narrowed, Jacques unyielding. "Your point?"

"Let me be clear. Any aid, any ships, any further attempted communication with Thólos, and I will bring a nightmare of horrors down upon you." Shepherd carelessly cracked his neck, his gaze steady upon the Commodore of Bernard Dome. "We men stand in a position to be comfortable allies. It would be unfortunate to miss an opportunity to work together to advance both our kingdoms over a *misunderstanding*."

Jacques was accustomed to court maneuverings, to dodging the knife in the back—not facing open threat to the front. But, it was not in his nature to acquiesce. He was Commodore, and had not become so by embracing weakness. That is why he ruled and his older brother was dead. "I will hear all your Ambassador has to say, while simultaneously reminding you that your ships' navigations will not function without my satellites. Your threats are impotent."

The Chancellor was prepared for such a statement. "Should communications go down, Bernard Dome would be riddled with plague in a matter of hours. The Red Consumption kills quickly, and you have nowhere to run."

The wall went dark.

With a snarl, Jacques turned on the silent Ambassador, gnashing his teeth as he demanded, "Explain!"

A shadowy smirk crossed Jules' lips, the very first expression he'd made since arrival. "Gladly."

❧

WAKING ALONE, Brenya found she'd overslept. A slight headache lingered as a reminder of the awful night before. Blinking tear-crusted eyes, she found it was more than her skull. Her body ached everywhere.

Jacques had been too rough with her over the couch. And his strange petting back in the room had not undone the damage.

But at least he had not made her... mate with him again. At least he had not turned her body against her and used the night hours to seek out her pleasure while taking everything he desired for his.

Jacques had done enough.

Sitting up in the bedding, Brenya looked at the white sea of soft things, a place he called her nest, and felt lonely beyond all measure.

He had not slept at her side; he had not woken her before he left. She should have felt some victory in the solitude, but after a lifetime with her Corps, Brenya was not accustomed to being alone.

It felt truly pathetic, but she brought up her knees and buried her face against them. Arms tight around her calves, trying to shut out the nest, the sunshine, and the memories, she cried.

Over the weeks in Jacques' care, all other tears had been out of fear or pain. This was the first time Brenya Perin had ever cried because she was sad.

The motion of it, the jagged inhales and messy

exhales… they were cathartic. Even soft wailing brought about its own sense of comfort until she was scrubbing her face with the heel of her hand beginning to calm.

She'd seen the look on Jacques' face last night. She'd found him watching her in the dark.

This was it for her. Termination.

He'd said it himself. *You are not the only Omega in Bernard Dome.*

The weight of his family's necklace was still fastened uncomfortably around her throat. It had to go. Fighting the clasp, she got the damn thing off, and left it lying on the sheets where it fell.

Whoever wore it next would fit this life better than she had. A real Omega, one who knew how to smile and what to say. One who would fawn over the Commodore, not shrink from him.

It was better that way, she supposed.

After a brief bath, the plainest clothing she could find was chosen. She washed her face, brushed her teeth, her hair, and walked out of Jacques Bernard's rooms. The cadre of guards at the door silently followed behind like a shadow. No soul in those busy halls tried to stop her when she found an exterior door, and pushed it open to step into the palace courtyard.

It struck her the second sun hit her face—this

was her first time outside beyond the breakfasts on Jacques' terrace.

It might be the last.

She did not know when he would end her misery. It did not seem his way to waste time, and if that were the case, there was one person she wanted to say goodbye to.

But George was not in Central. And Brenya knew without a doubt that she would not be permitted in Beta Sector. He'd have to come to her.

COMstations dotted clean cobblestone streets. Rushing toward the nearest one, wondering why she had not thought to do this before, she knew a brief lightness of spirit.

"Unit 512XT." All she had to do was speak his designation and the computers would handle the rest. Palms sweating, she held her breath, exhaling in a whoosh when a familiar face appeared on the screen. "George!"

The Beta was surprised, adjusting his glasses as if they were malfunctioning. "We were told you were grounded and reassigned to Central."

Nodding, she grew breathless, grinning stupidly. "Yes. I'm in Central. Can you come here? Can you come now?"

The Beta replied immediately, "Affirmative, Unit 17C."

"I lost my designation when he brought me here, George. I'm nothing but Brenya Perin now."

It took him twenty minutes to travel the distance to Central's gate, three minutes to clear through the line. When he stood before her, eyeing her odd clothing with confusion, Brenya threw her arms around him and clung as if he might save her again.

He couldn't, she knew that.

But it felt good to hold a real friend.

20

I t started with a video feed of panicked Thólos Enforcers locked behind contamination control. No detail was missed: blood streaming from eyes, noses, and mouths of all those scratching at the sealed door to get out. Screams. The begging to any Gods who might listen. Jacques watched the whole unedited thing the entire hour it took for thousands of people to die in agony before incineration protocol turned their bodies to dust.

"The Red Consumption spares no one." Ambassador Jules changed the display to that of war torn streets. "Panic ensued, riots breaking out immediately. In less than a day, Shepherd had control of the city. We allowed his 'martial law'. We allowed the rabid population to act as it would." Images were rotating over the wall, horrific things all with the soundtrack of wails and shrieks. "The people of Thólos killed each other while we watched. The crowds cheered when their own Senators were hung. They thanked Shepherd for each new horror. What they did, they did to themselves."

Like his father, and his father before him, Jacques had studied the effects of the Red Consumption and the Reformation Wars. He had seen ancient images of the virus in action, read medical reports, understood exactly the effect it had on a human body, but he had never seen anything like this. It was sobering, the cold creeping reality of so menacing a threat. "And your Chancellor who would be my ally has brought this to my Dome."

Jules was quick to counter. "We have no interest in doing your people harm. But, it is imperative that you see this and that you understand why Thólos must be left to rot. Decadence at the cost of those who are weakest will always lead to revolution. You can only torment your people for so long before they rise up against you."

"There is no tyranny in Bernard Dome. The population is controlled, passive, fulfilled, and thriving"—Jacques' fury was held behind a stone cold gaze—"as you have seen for yourself."

"Chemical constraint is an ingenious way of managing the baser human urges. Shepherd is very interested in this technique. I believe if you were to share your knowledge with him, he would be grateful. Prisons, as your forbearer knew, are ineffective." Jules operated the massive COMscreen's controls to offer more data, more images, more gore for the viewing of those poor souls collected in the room. "Your proletariat class is indeed thriving, workers completely unaware that they are laboring for Centrist luxuries. Central in itself is an interesting place... you have created your own snake pit, which does not concern us at all. Petty rivalries, grasps for power... such childishness will happen anywhere. We did not come here to emancipate your slave class or to punish your inept treatment of females."

Jules had crossed a line; Jacques growing before him as he spat, "Females are protected and cherished here. Our laws are extensive!"

The Beta Ambassador did not flinch, but he did slide his gaze from the Commodore to his silent and seething Security Advisor in the corner. "I stand corrected."

Ancil growled.

The insult would not stand. Not after the extortion and Shepherd's rudeness. Jacques had his own threats to make. "I am tempted to have you and each of your Omegas immediately executed."

It was Ancil who stepped forward. Ancil who smelled of fear and outright challenge. "What would the females have known? They are only women. Lucia should not be held accountable for this fool's—"

Jules raised his hand, cutting off the alarmed Alpha to address the Commodore. "You may have us executed. Shepherd will not retaliate for such a response. I guarantee, were he in your position, he would have already ordered our deaths—they would have been public and they would have been painful. That is your choice, but I have been instructed to make certain you understand his only interest is in your potential actions concerning Thólos. What happens under Bernard Dome is none of his concern. What lessons you may take from what I've shown you are yours to decide. Could what happened in Thólos happen here? I don't know. I don't care. That would be your problem to solve."

He had a great deal to consider and this was not the place for deliberation. Jacques spoke his ruling, "You are no longer allowed free rein of the palace or city, Ambassador Havel. You are to remain quarantined on your ship. You will not be granted clearance to leave until I have made my decision regarding your neck."

Offering a bow, Jules accepted the terms. "As you say."

Cutting a glance to Ancil, Jacques ordered,

"Lucia is to be under house arrest. The remaining Omegas will remain in confinement."

Ancil was not appeased. Not one bit. "She's pregnant with my child, Jacques."

Colder than ice, Jacques turned his back on his friend and moved toward the door. "You already have a son and heir."

BRENYA'S MEETING with George had been short, the pair having little time to do more than sit on a retaining wall near the gate and speak quietly with one another—if they spoke at all. Comfortable silence was more soothing than answering questions, and George had never been the talkative type.

But she had given him one stern warning. "Do not do anything that might risk your reassignment."

Confusion wrinkled the skin between George's eyes. "Are you unfulfilled with your newest assignment?"

"There is no assignment. Do you understand what I'm saying?" Huffing out frustration in an attempt to quash the ache in her heart, Brenya added, "There is no new assignment no matter your skill set or service record. There is no mercy, George. That's why I wanted to say goodbye today. I needed to thank you for everything. I could not have asked for a better tech. I know you're the reason I wasn't cut from the rigging."

"I knew you would climb up. You always do." He seemed oblivious to the praise. "It has been nice to confirm you are well. Now, I must report for duty."

She could see it in his mannerisms, in the way he replied. She must have been just like him a few short weeks ago. Robotic. "Of course. Thank you for making time to visit me."

"You smell very appealing at this moment." George stood, adjusting his jumpsuit and offering a salute. "I would be interested in submitting a mating invoice, if you were amenable. I have leave for mental hygiene in three days."

Brenya blinked. She could think of nothing to say beyond, "I will be unavailable. My apologies, Unit 512XT."

The Beta turned to leave with no further formality. He turned to leave as if he had no idea what had transpired. How could he know? How could he know anything protected as he was with fulfilling work and chemical-laced beta rations that made a simple life meaningful.

Waiting until he cleared the line and was out of her sight forever, Brenya whispered, "Goodbye, George. Thank you for being my friend."

One of the massive Alpha guards shadowing

Brenya interrupted her reverie. "You are drawing undo attention and should return to the palace now. We have orders to limit your exposure to crowds."

Glassy-eyed, Brenya brought her head up. There were strangers, mostly male, edging closer and sniffing. More than one had an obvious erection.

George had not meant to make her feel unclean with his request to mate, but it had been a reminder of why Jacques kept her as his pet. Omegas only had one purpose: an Alpha's pleasure. Finding utter strangers eyeing her, knowing what they wanted, how they would use her, made the inevitable end of the day more bearable.

Who would want to live like this?

How did those pretty butterflies from Greth tolerate it? Maybe it had been different for Omegas in their Dome. If so, those poor women were set to be disappointed.

Maybe they liked the attention.

Brenya would rather not have strangers staring at her, their eyes looking at her chest and gawking at the hidden slit between her legs.

If one of them growled, she'd vomit.

The guard was right; she did not belong there. There was no single place in Bernard Dome she fit.

Marching in the opposite direction of the gate, Brenya found her guards decisively handled those who would follow... though one male required restraint. Beginning to understand why Jacques had ordered so many to watch her, she kept moving, walking aimlessly as fast as she could as if she might leave everything behind.

She had no idea where she was going, hardly cared so long as she was in the sun and free of Jacques' pretty things and soft bed. Someone else would be in that nest soon, so there was no use in feeling any sense of loss.

There was no reason to be melancholy.

She'd seen her friend. She'd gone outside. She should not be feeling tears fall down her cheeks.

Except she was.

She was softly crying, wandering a segment of the city she did not know at all, with absolutely no place to go.

Why did it have to be such a beautiful day? Had she been making *the descent*, her bio-suit would have been heated by sunshine, there would have been a light breeze rocking her in the rigging. It would have been heaven.

With her heart so low, the weather should have been dreary, rain slapping against the side of the Dome to blur the view of the distant ruins outside.

For a moment she was furious with George for breaking protocol all those weeks ago. Had they cut her from the rigging, she would have died without ever knowing this place, Bernard secrets… what she was. She could have died with honor to be remembered by Palo Corps, not grounded in shame, waiting to be terminated for failure to adequately serve the Commodore's physical needs.

You are not the only Omega in Bernard Dome.

Someone else would soon know what he tasted like... he might even be with one of them now. Someone else would be blasted to pieces when the *little death* came to cull its price. Someone else would tangle their hands in his soft hair and see him smile.

Someone else would be called *mon chou*.

Jacques' words last night had cut her deeper than he'd ever know.

Someone else would be hurt by him.

And Brenya could do nothing... because she would be dead. Annette would never coach another Omega on how to please the Commodore, because she would be a cog enslaved to raising a brood of children she had desired for herself.

Which one of them had it worse?

Annette did.

And Jacques had allowed that to happen. The same Jacques who twisted up her insides when he called her beautiful despite her mutilated face. The same Jacques who terrified her when he held her down and forced her to feel him.

It would almost be better if she didn't have to

see the Alpha before termination took place. One look at her weeping in the streets of his kingdom, and he'd know he'd won.

He would know that sometimes... sometimes when he touched her it had been beautiful beyond all measure. He would know that she'd hated not waking up in his arms even though she despised what he was.

And that... that was the most horrifying part of it all.

21

How she'd wound up on the tarmac, Brenya didn't know. She had no clue what part of Central she was in, how far the palace might be... but staring at the massive ship waiting there, she found she could not bring herself to care.

It was beautiful, sun glinting off the silver solar collection panels just as it would have off Bernard Dome's siding. The sight was so familiar and so alien all at once.

Without hesitation, her hand reached out, finger-tips tracing over the lines of the hull. The metal was warm. Warm enough to take the chill from her bones. Warm enough to distract a lost woman from her troubles.

With a sniff, she paced around the monstrosity,

knowing what it must be: Ambassador Jules Havel's ship.

As far as Brenya knew, there were no aerial craft in Bernard Dome. Or, if there were, she'd never been exposed to them. And this one was an original from the Reformation Wars. There were scars in the hull and marks where turrets must have once been attached.

This was a treasure, a living piece of history... and she was touching it.

When she rounded the back and found the gang-plank down and hatch open, mindlessly she abandoned her guard and let her explorations take her inside.

The cargo ship could hold a great deal but was practically empty, little more than a few chairs bolted into the floor. There were no comforts, no niceties, a solitary cot set up in the corner and a room near the flight deck rigged for human waste disposal.

It was perfect. Completely perfect.

The nearest metal sheeting access panel was easy to remove, opening up a fascinating view of the guts of the craft. The upper part of her body bent into the crevice, Brenya spoke to the wiring, the pipes, the generator coils, listing what they were as if she had built the machine herself. "Vandigrath magnetic couplings. Coolant housing. Electrical flight circuitry."

"What do you think you're doing?"

Ambassador Havel had not been there when she'd arrived, or if he had, he'd hidden out of sight. Gone was his cold tone, the one he'd used to interrupt her explorations bearing the hiss of acid chewing through metal instead.

It might have been because there was nothing left to lose, but the Beta's open aggression did nothing to her. Brenya continued her explorations even as she replied, "Your ship is... remarkable. I have studied old schematics, but I've never seen one intact."

Jules' tone dropped lower. "Remove yourself from there immediately, or I will remove you."

"Why?" Her hand had been fingering a mismatching link of tubing. Closing her fist about a crusted red hose, she yanked hard enough to rip it from its nest.

He'd moved faster than her eyes could track, slamming her body against the wall, his forearm across her throat.

Total shock was on her face, in her scent, expediting the rise and fall of her chest.

Showing his teeth, Jules was much more animated than she'd ever witnessed. "What did you damage?"

The sound of sand falling on the floor increased when she held up the spoiled tubing and met those chilling eyes. "This is a size seven cycle regulator hose. Had you tried to take flight with the accumulating crystals blocking the tubing, your energy converter would have redlined and your ship would have crashed in minutes. Whoever replaced this should never have used a plastics lined connector. It must be silicone. The subsequent chemical reaction destroyed the internal structure. I'm amazed you even made it all the way here."

Narrowing his lids, the man's bright blue eyes darted down to see what she held in her grip and the subsequent mess it was making on the floor. "How would you know that?"

She knew it because she was once the best engineering grunt under the Dome. Growing angry at the injustice of it all, tired of being pushed around by males, Brenya growled—she growled in the exact manner Jacques had told her not to. "If you tried to take off without repairing this mistake, you would die. Rerouting existing tubing would take me less than three minutes. Do you want me to fix it, or do you want to dispose of me?"

"Dispose?" Her word choice seemed to upend the Beta, who backed away while looking her over. Like all the others, his eyes found the scar. "Far be it from me to harm those with good intentions."

If it was supposed to be a joke, she didn't get it. Dropping the damaged tube, she turned her back on the threat and went to work. As she said, it took three minutes to rig a bypass with original parts. "Your thrust will be decreased, but at least you won't fall out of the sky."

By the time she had finished threading the tubing into place, there was engine grease smeared on her hands and her clothing. The smell was familiar and comforting, the slippery feeling between her fingers pleasant.

Her sleeves were made all the worse when she rolled them up so they would not catch as she dived forward to test the connections.

The ship was powered down, but she could cycle the fluids by flipping a series of switches, intuitively knowing what to manipulate and exactly how much force to use.

When it was done, she straightened, creeping back to face the looming Beta. "Repairs are complete."

Arms crossed over his chest, he scowled at her. First it was her hands, then the mottled bruises on her forearms, those blue eyes lingering over the worst ones at her wrist. He gave her the luxury of skipping over her chest and going right back to the puckered scar on her face.

Turning her head so he might only see her good

cheek, she scanned for more access panels, eager to open them up and see what she might find. "I would like to—"

Ignoring her half-formed request, Jules asked, "Did the Commodore cut your face?"

Brenya kept her head turned and eyes anywhere but on him. "No. While making repairs to a damaged solar collector, my rigging failed. I fell down the side of the Dome. During the accident my helmet's visor shattered," she whispered, adding the worst part of her secret, "I breathed outside air."

The male hardly blinked an eye. "I see."

Dirty fingers untucked the hair from behind her ear, drawing the locks forward as if to cover her face. "I am aware the disfigurement is off-putting. Omegas are supposed to be beautiful."

"Omegas are supposed to be people."

There had been no inflection behind his phrasing. It was just a blunt statement, but something about hearing so simple a declaration made Brenya shyly turn her head to face him, horribly scarred cheek and all.

She didn't know what to say, she didn't know why those words seemed important, she just wanted to look in his eyes and see if he was lying.

It was hard to tell.

"May I explore your ship further? I can catalogue any required repairs your diagnostic programs may have missed."

Steps sounded on the gangplank, a familiar aggressive scent preceding the massive body of the last person Brenya wanted to see.

"I have been looking for you, *mon chou*." Narrowing his eyes, Jacques looked over her messy clothing, glancing next to the nearby Beta before announcing in a voice that was not one bit pleased. "How strange to find you here."

Her heart sank. It would have been nice to spend a few hours enjoying the craft before he took her away and ended her life. Wiping her hands on her skirt, she cast her eyes to the floor. "Hello, Jacques."

Jules' open disdain was cruel, the Beta mocking her before the Alpha. "Your Omega has taken it upon herself to pull my ship apart."

An ironic chuckle, then a hint of darkness layered the statement as Jacques purred the words, "It seems she's had quite the adventure today."

Her earlier bravery was gone. Swallowing, she pleaded, "I'm not ready yet…"

She was not ready to die. Not yet.

"Then, by all means, play to your heart's content." Taking the nearest jump seat, Jacques crossed an ankle over his knee and motioned for her to continue. "The Ambassador's ship isn't going anywhere anytime soon."

She must have misheard him, Brenya glancing back and forth between the two males staring one another down. Taking a cautious step toward a floor panel she assumed covered the hover mechanics, no one stopped her. When she reached down to pry it open, not a word was said.

Ancient machinery was at her fingertips, the extremely complicated mechanics making her fingertips twitch in anticipation of all she could learn. She dove in, willing to seize the distraction for as long as it was offered.

In a matter of minutes, a collection of parts had been organized around the floor, Brenya working to see what type of energy coupler the old ship employed. She found something much more interesting. There was an insignia on the hull hidden under decades of murk.

It read Thólos.

Cocking her head, she wiped it clean, certain her eyes must be wrong.

Thólos, clear as day.

The Ambassador's ship had not come from Greth Dome.

Glancing up, she locked eyes with Jacques.

He asked her point blank, "Did you find anything interesting?"

Yes, she had. "Everything about this ship is interesting."

22

H and at her back, Jacques led his quiet Omega down the more picturesque Central pathways toward the palace. It had grown dark in the hours he'd let her play at deconstructing the prick Ambassador's ship, leaving the streets aglow with soft light playing over the old European architecture of surrounding buildings. The Dome had done well capturing the spirit of all that had been lost, tree lined streets, canals, a reflection of dead cities compressed into one space.

All of this was lost on Brenya.

She was quiet, shoulders drooping and eyes missing the beauty. Withdrawn, she dragged her feet and kept their steps slow.

Jacques didn't like it. He wanted her as she had

been elbow deep reassembling whatever she'd taken apart. "You enjoyed yourself working on the ship."

For a split second he saw her face grow wistful. One blink and it was gone, her expression as detached as her words. "I did. It was nice to remember that once I had been more than…"

"Than what?"

She screwed up her brow as if unsure how to phrase her thoughts. "Something inadequate. I was an excellent engineering grunt. I am not skilled in any of my new tasks."

He halted their steps, smirking with a mind full of indecent thoughts. "On that, we'll have to disagree."

His teasing did not lighten her brooding at all. If anything, it only made her appear more miserable. "How much farther is it? I will comply and remain obedient, but I am growing anxious. I'd like it to be over soon."

Jade eyes narrowed. "Explain."

Her lips shook, honey eyes casting about as if they might find something to keep her steady. "If I asked you to purr while they do it, would you?"

"You, girl, are frustrating beyond all measure."

She wrapped her dirty arms around her grease-stained middle as if she might hold whatever she was feeling inside. "I know. I am an unsatisfactory Omega."

This was his fault. He had been careless in his vanity and cruel in his temper. Angry with more than himself, he stated, "You believe I am taking you to be terminated."

Her voice caught, but she was brave enough to turn pretty eyes up and meet the gaze of the male she thought was to have her killed. "I'm not the only Omega under the Dome."

He put a finger to her chest, tapping it on her breastbone. "And which Omega would replace you?"

"The blonde female was very beautiful. She made you laugh."

Dry, he quipped, "I was notified that she entered the early stages of estrous this morning. I could pair-bond with her immediately."

"That..." Brenya blinked, exhaled, then offered, "is convenient. I'm sure you will be happy."

Scoffing, he shook his head. "You have honestly considered this, haven't you?" The corner of Jacques' lips curled, equally pitiless and amused. "I was under the impression that only seasoned wives thought to tell an Alpha male what to do."

The word *wives* shut her down. "Will you purr like I asked? I would appreciate it if you started now."

Anticipating a different reaction from the female, Jacques sighed. On his next breath he did begin to purr. Seeing the small thing's immediate relief, he reached out, took her face in his hands, and watched her eyelids droop. Smoothing a thumb over her trembling lip, he murmured, "Last night was unpleasant, but I did not intend this to be your reaction."

He'd been working to inspire jealousy, not fear for her life. The whole show after dinner had been to make her desire him more—the laughing with the females, the prodding of her pride. He should have known better. Brenya Perin was not wired that way.

Instead *she* had made him insanely jealous— seeing the feed of her talking with the scrawny Beta pushing him past the pale. She had even dared to throw her arms around the man. She had dared to smile when he'd talked.

Perhaps he had overreacted. The earlier meeting with Shepherd had been a blow. Knowing the Dome was under an invisible siege, and that in a very real sense his hands were tied, burned his ego. Brenya's naiveté and innocence burned him more. "What if I do not desire to terminate you?"

The magic of his purr could not change the look of terror when her eyes flew open. "I don't want to be given to another Alpha." Throat, flexing, color draining from her face… Brenya looked on the cusp of being ill. "I can't imagine another person… on me."

That appeased him somewhat. "That won't happen."

She took a shaky breath, nodding. A tear even dared to fall from her eye. "What is going to happen to me then?"

"You're going to learn how to handle my temper." He reached to stroke her hair, purring all the louder. "I'm going to work on choosing my words when I'm angry. And I am still angry… as I am sure you sense. You acted against your best interests today, and I took action to prevent it in the future, but we will discuss that later. Right now we are going to walk back to our nest. I'm going to feed you dinner, and we will relax. And then I am going to mount you. It will be rough. I can't bring myself to be gentle, because you have been rebellious and I need to see you punished. But I promise you, when you come, your screams will be those of bliss, not pain." He set his lips to her forehead, pulling his sweet, unyielding mate into his arms. "Tonight, you will learn the difference between rape and discipline."

Her scent changed, fear fading into something hinging closer to excitement. "Will you sleep in the nest when you're done with me?"

"I promise my knot will be inside you. There may be very little sleep, though. I intend to be thorough for both our sakes."

SWEAT MATTED her hair to her head, Brenya unable to catch her breath.

Looming over her, the Alpha glared down, an expression of perfect violence playing off the joy of his conquest. "What did you learn?"

That he could do so much more to her than she knew. Moaning as her insides throbbed, Brenya grimaced, unable to speak.

He tweaked her nipple pulling it upward until her ribcage bowed. He smiled. "What did you learn, *mon chou*?"

It should have hurt, a great many of the things he had done to her had... but it did not. Not anymore. When he released the puckered flesh, and took its twin to offer the same treatment, she swooned.

Soft, timbre exceedingly gentle, Jacques said, "You are more beautiful in this moment than I have ever seen you."

Lashes parting, she found his blurred form glowed. Dreamlike waves of warmth moved over her weighted limbs. She tried to move them, having forgotten he had chained her to the bed.

That had been the first step in his lesson. She was at his mercy, always.

The *roughness* he had threatened her with was

more in theory than in practice, though he had abused her slit when the rut made him frantic in the first knotting of the night. Afterward, he had pulled out and brought down his hand against the fleshier parts of her skin: buttocks, thighs, even between her legs until she'd climaxed.

Her body had surprised her, and he had grinned when abundant slick squished out between his fingers. His cock had not even been inside her.

Jacques had lowered himself over her, his lips whispering at her ear, "Don't you care for me even a little? Would you come like that for any male? Did you come like that for George?"

"No…"

He thumbed her clit until her legs began to shake. "No to which question?"

The kind of noise that fought its way out of her body was a squeal that both pled for mercy and wanted more. "I never came with George! I never knew this feeling!"

"And how about this one?" His fingers slipped inside, hooking behind her pubic bone. He pressed up against that fleshy place, kneading it until she grew red from holding her breath as if to escape.

Somehow he drew a jet of slick, catching it in his hand to bring to his own swollen body part. Working her juices up and down his shaft, he cocked his head… waiting for her to recover enough to torment further. "Yet, you went to the Beta today. You touched him as you should only touch me. You smiled."

His colder tone broke through her delirium, Brenya sucking in a breath and releasing a shaking answer, "I wanted to say goodbye. He saved my life."

"He did not save your life." Jacques jerked her body, made her conform to the shape of his hips as his cockhead butted against her opening. Shoving in with an animal grunt, he'd roared. "I did."

Blasted apart, she bucked, eager for more.

"You would have been terminated had I not found you. You would have been lost to me forever! I SAVED YOU. What thanks do I get?" He spread her legs so far they began to burn, screaming at the overwrought female. "Suspicion? Coldness? You have been ungrateful."

She wanted so badly to rake her fingernails across his rippling abdominals, to sink her teeth into him. Salivating, she squeezed down, using the only muscles she had control over to make him feel her frustration.

His eyes rolled back, the knot threatening to expand at his base, forcing him to stop all movement. "Not yet. Not until I say, bad girl."

"WHY!" She growled, vicious, rabid, and completely beyond control.

She could try to wriggle and feed his cock deeper inside her, but the chains binding her arms above her head would only let her stretch so far. He put a stop to it, his hands pinning her hips to the bed.

"What did I tell you about growling at a male?"

Throwing her head back and forth, she refused to listen, her body cramping in its need for release. "I don't care."

She was panting, and he was asking her questions. It wasn't fair.

"What did you learn?"

She learned that she didn't want him to stop anymore, that anything was better than loneliness and the long walk toward termination.

"If you give me a satisfactory answer, Brenya, I will give you everything you need and more."

It was easy to see past emotion when her body had demands. In that moment, it was easy to be Omega. "I learned that I did not like waking up alone. I hated it more than I hated wearing the diamonds. I hated it more than being humiliated at your dinner. I hated it more than your cruelty toward Annette."

Excitement lit his eyes, Jacques' voice husky as he demanded, "Why?"

"Because I knew what it meant." Her nerves were still on edge, tremors wracking her body as if the little death was knocking at her door, and this time would take more than just a piece of her soul. It would defeat her utterly. "It meant that I was nothing but what Ancil had said. A toy. And that I had been displayed for your amusement, then discarded when no longer valuable. My opinion meant nothing to you. My skills worthless. I was reduced to a hole you could fuck and was soon to be replaced."

"Your unflappable honesty is... extraordinary." The Alpha's muscles tensed, his cheek twitching as he held her immobile and said, "A simple 'I learned there are consequences when I misbehave' would have been sufficient."

She had made him angry. That seemed to be her best talent these days. "You will choose another Omega."

"You would presume again to tell me what I will do. You refuse to listen." A low growl, a deep resounding warning preceded, "How can I make you obey?"

A slow slide of his hips and he pulled almost all the way from the heat of her body and ever so slowly inched back in. "I could fuck you. I am fucking you. I can bend your body to my will, but your mind refuses. Maybe I should have had another Alpha take what he would. That way you could compare my love to his lust. Would you submit to me then when I came to scoop you from his nest and save you? Would you love me if you'd felt what it truly was to be used? I could not bring myself to do it, though last night I came precariously close."

Her mind wanted to melt into the mattress, to escape from him when he spoke in such a way, but her body was a traitorous slut. Rocking her hips to his new, sluggish tempo, she followed where the Alpha would lead—lost, ruined, and desperate.

"You look very sweet while you sleep. It's easy to forget how gullible and hardheaded you are." Setting his finger to her clit, watching her body be dominated by such pitiless tactics, he cooed, "And then you reached for where I should have lain by your side. You reached for me even after all your refusals and accusations. Somewhere in this body of yours, you know I already own you. The pair-bond is only a formality."

He kept her teetering on the edge to the point she could hardly comprehend words. All Brenya could grasp in that moment were actions. His actions were more often deceitful than not. A whispered moan, her eyes closing, and a smile on her mouth, Brenya said, "You're a liar, Jacques Bernard."

Chuckling, he angled in such a way that made her fluids squish out and drip down his sack. "Smiling as you misbehave will not spare you the rod. In fact, I think you want to be punished, and that is not behavior I wish to encourage. Be a good girl now. Tell me you're sorry."

"For what?"

The chains rattled, the mechanism to release clicking. "This will not do, *mon chou*."

Her hands were free, but before she might enjoy it, he rolled their bodies and set her in a position that woke her from the mating high's stupor. He was prone under her body while still inside her. She was on top, braced against his chest and taking him so deep she could hardly bear it.

His hands were not guiding her movement, in fact, they lay innocently at his sides. There was no stopping what her body did, how it wriggled and pulsed until Brenya began to move up and down his shaft. She had no clue what she was doing or why. Her head fell back, her hair brushing her spine as she took what she needed so she might know release.

He'd threatened her with bliss and here it was. It was hers, on her terms, and so close the first ripples of her tunnel were already squeezing his shaft.

"Wall unit, order four."

He'd spoken and she'd ignored, caught up in the freedom to take. Desperate cries filled the air, the most obscene of moans... so fucking loud it took her a moment to realize they were not hers.

Eyes opening, she found one wall had come alive with a view of a familiar blonde Omega screaming release, forcing Brenya's own to clench and take her.

"MORE! Gods it's not enough! Fuck me harder."

There was a man between that woman's legs, a man pounding away with abandon. He was skinny and his glasses were gone, crying out his frustration in a voice Brenya had heard day after day in her ear.

A war broke out inside her gut, the milking clenching of orgasm breaking over muscle and bone, twisted up in a mind that began to grasp what Jacques had done… what he was showing her.

This was her punishment.

Tearing her eyes from the perversion on the wall, feeling his knot tie them together, coming despite it all, she turned a betrayed gaze to Jacques.

He smiled. "Does she look satisfied to you? I'd say not. The scrawny Beta could never give you this."

A wave of come shot from him, blasting her insides. She groaned and bent against her will. She could not stop the *little death* even in a moment as awful as this.

Hand on her belly, Jacques traced his name on her skin, the vulgar sound of her friend crying out a pained release filling the air. "I find that I am a jealous man after all, Brenya. Take it to heart. Any male you touch, I'll take their hand—if you smile at them, their tongue. Your smiles, your touches, I want them all to myself. If you give me that, I will let your George live after the Omega is done with him."

In moments of crisis, the human body could do miraculous things. She may have been tied to him by the knot, under his power in every way, but her hand drew back and formed a fist.

Shrieking, Brenya struck him with all the strength of her being.

Over, and over, and over.

23

Tape had been wrapped over her split knuckles. Jacques had put it there. He had kissed the wounds tenderly making sure each little cut had been cleaned and covered. He had taken such care of her, one would think he was the gentle, loving man he pretended to be.

She'd given him a black eye, a bloody nose, and a bruise on his jaw. He wore them like a badge of honor.

In fact, he seemed to be very proud of his fractured female.

The wall was silent, the picture of George fucking an unsatisfied blonde Omega gone, but it was burned in her mind forever.

Brenya had thrown up.

It had not happened until after he'd caught her

hands and held them before her. It had not happened until the full measure of his knot receded and what he'd put inside her gushed out. Gingerly, he'd lifted the struck woman... the one who could hardly breathe... pulled his cock from her, and set her beside him on the bed.

She was like a puppet, she didn't fight. She hardly even blinked.

When he'd gone to brush her hair from her face, she'd doubled over and ruined the bedding.

"I know it was harsh." Rubbing her back, he let her heave, unconcerned with the mess. "Punishment is not supposed to be pleasant."

A small voice dared, "Why would you do that to him?"

"He asked your permission to submit a mating invoice so he could fuck you just as I did." The man's voice grew disgusted. "Since he *saved your life,* as you believe, I spared his. I was even generous enough to grant his modified request. Gabriella... the blonde Omega you thought to foist on me... will have some small relief in estrous. When all is said and done, your tech will not think of you in lust again. He'll think of her."

Brenya could not bring herself to raise her head. "Are you going to have him terminated?"

"Don't contact him again, Brenya, and you'll never need worry about his health." His arm slipped under her knees, Jacques pressing her to his chest so he might stand. "Come now. You need a bath. It will make you feel better."

And bathe her he had, just as Annette had done not so long ago.

Through it all he purred, and pet, and told her she was loved. She was not once chastised for striking him, though he clucked over the wounds.

When he carried her back into the bedroom, fresh bedding already awaited. Locked in his arms she was made to lie down, facing the opposite wall where she'd seen the horror, and blinking in the dark.

Jacques sang her a lullaby, stroking her arm with the back of his fingers. It might have been his voice, the purr, the sweep of his fingers... it might have been utter mental and physical exhaustion... but Brenya grew still.

She could not bear to think, pretending instead that she was taking apart the engine of the cargo ship again. That was a safe place... the Thólosen ship brought here by a Greth Ambassador.

She was going insane.

Staring straight ahead, a hollow voice sought answers. "You told me that Thólos fell. What happened there?" *Why was one of their ships in Bernard Dome?*

Turning her to face him, the Commodore put her ear to his chest. "What a question for this hour."

"I don't understand the world at all."

He began to stroke her hair, kissing her crown as he swore, "I'll keep you safe from the world. Your innocence is beautiful, and I'd rather you never know what has become of that place or the people who live there."

"Live?" Brenya wanted more. She wanted answers. She wanted anything that might tie that ship to a way out. "You said they were all dead."

The man grumbled, closing his eyes for sleep. "Their Dome is cracked, exposing survivors to the elements. Soon they will be."

How would one repair a cracked Dome? That was a question Brenya could answer in exact detail.

The Alpha beast began to snore.

Flexing her sore fists, she dared to think forbidden thoughts and let her mind run wild with the fantasy that very well could be a reality... if she dared to slowly reach for the shackles left lying on the sheets.

She was never going to survive this. She had to get away from him. She had to get out.

There was a faint click as she closed the first around his wrist. The male's second arm was much more difficult. It took her an hour to feign organic movement that turned his body to meld with hers.

And then it was done. He was chained as she had been.

Scooting away, heart in her throat, she parroted his words from earlier, "Wall unit, order four."

The desperate moans of the Omega in heat had grown even louder, as had George's grunts as he thrust like a maniac. Jacques' eyes flew open. It only took him a moment to recognize what she had done.

"*Mon chou*, I strongly suggest—"

She stuffed a wad of bedding in his mouth, tearing at the soft fabric so he would not be able to easily spit it out.

One strong yank on the chains, and he found he could not bring his hands together to unlatch them. Roaring behind the gag, Jacques went wild, shaking the bed with such force that Brenya flew back and pressed her naked body to the wall.

No one would hear him over the sounds of manic sex, but it was only a matter of time before he broke the bed frame.

Scrambling to enact a reckless and poorly thought out plan, she took his clock and smashed it on the floor. From the wreckage she scooped up the largest cog, some broken metal fragments, anything she might use as a tool. Two minutes later, she had the ventilation panel parted from the wall and was scrambling like a rat through the air ducts.

He would not be able to follow through so tight

a passage, not that it gave her courage. She knew when he broke free, his wrath would come down upon her like a hammer. There would be no talk or punishments. It would be the true end.

One way or another tonight was the last time he'd twist her with his games.

It was dark in the city, but the pink tinged refraction on the glass warned dawn would be breaking soon. An unclothed female would draw attention. Fortunately, ventilation went everywhere, the paths intuitive to someone who'd spent years maintaining them.

She made remarkable time back to the Thólosen ship. It was almost too easy.

The gangplank had sealed, and she didn't know the access codes to open it. It was sacrilegious to damage such a perfect machine, but Brenya pried open the mechanics and crossed wires that would make the door surge. She only needed it to unhinge enough to squeeze through, throwing her body weight against the hatch until it gave.

Straining to pry it one more inch apart, Brenya plunked her bare foot to the hull. With just enough leverage she was able to lift her body to where the gap was widest and fall gracelessly inside the ship.

The hatch sealed behind her, leaving her in the dark.

She did not need to see to remember where the

cockpit lay. She ran, she ran as if the ship was hers, built by her hands and yipped in triumph when her hands found the shape of a door.

The lever was thrown, mechanics whirring, and then she was there, looking over the controls, just as the sun broke the horizon.

"You'll never get out, you know."

Screaming, Brenya rounded on the voice, holding out the sharp edge of a cog as if it might save her.

On the other side of the cargo door was nothing more than the shine of eyes in the dark. The Ambassador was there, watching, easing closer by the second.

It could not end this way, not after what she'd done. "You weren't supposed to be in here."

His voice was steady, the complete opposite of her high pitched panic. "The same could be said about you."

Flying forward to catch the door before he might reach her, she threw it closed and jammed the lock.

She didn't have time to think through her actions, she had to get the ship off the ground. These things were built to fly themselves, but they could not take off without manual control—just as she would not be able to exit the Dome without overriding the passcodes.

In the captain's chair she gave herself a moment

to look over the knobs, buttons, levers, and stick. Machines made sense, she understood their language better than the spoken word, and reached forward to flip a red toggle.

The engine shuddered, thrust coming online. There was only one bay the ship might have fit through, and she knew exactly where it was. Jerking the stick, she threw the ship into the sky, Brenya overcorrecting before she upended the vessel. Her next attempt was smoother and then glass was all that separated her from a Dome full of lies, and air that smelled of jasmine.

Codes were entered, codes she should never have known but had picked up over years of making *the descent*. The panels parted and she shot out of Bernard Dome and into freedom.

Brenya smiled.

She smiled despite the sound of a man attacking the door at her back. The Beta would not get through that much metal... not unless he knew how to take it apart.

He didn't.

24

She flew south according to the instruments on the dash, the sun climbing a horizontal path around her ship. Hours ago the man had stopped trying to force open the door, and she had calmed, surrounded by the subsequent sound of the surrounding mechanics functioning in harmony.

At midday, a meadow was found that would offer sufficient room for the ship to land and recharge solar energy cells. The remainder of the flying would have to take place at night. Either way, Bernard Dome was far behind her. She would not even know how to find it if she turned around.

The thought was extremely comforting.

When the ship came to a standstill and the whir of energy collection replaced engine noise, there was a knock at the door.

Swiveling in the chair, Brenya looked at the barrier between her and her unexpected hostage. She had to talk to him, owed him an explanation.

She could rig the door to only open a few inches, and debated through another series of knocks on the wisdom of such an enterprise.

It was not his fault she had done something extreme.

It was not his fault at all.

Her hands began to shake again as she fiddled with the mechanics, making the simple adjustment take twice as long as it should. When she pressed the button and the hydraulics hissed, she crossed her arms over her chest, less out of modesty and more out of needing the comfort of her own arms.

Unsure what to say to him, Brenya stood and found the quick shine of his eyes in the dark.

"Aren't you going to let me in?"

She let her head fall into her hand, finding it harder to speak than she'd expected. "I've altered ignition programming... you can't fly the ship without flipping the switches in an exact order. A mistake will blow the system. If by some miracle you got in here, you need me alive, or this is where we stay forever."

His voice was as dead as the world around them. "I don't imagine you understand the weight of what you've done."

Shaking her head, she rubbed the grit from her cheeks. "I had to get out."

"Naked?"

She couldn't help her lack of dress. "This is a Thólosen vessel."

The shine of his eyes never wavered. "Yes."

"Why do you have it?"

"I was born in Thólos."

"Good." Without the engines heating the craft, she began to shiver from the growing chill. "That's where I'm going. Once I have arrived, I will give the ship back to you. You can take it wherever you wish."

Even with darkness shadowing his face, Brenya knew the man smiled. It was not a friendly grin. Neither was his rejoinder. "I can't let you do that."

She had never spoken with such open rebellion in her life. It felt good. "I'm not asking you. It was not my intention to take you with me, but you are my hostage; I am not yours."

"And when you get there?" Jules eyed her lack of clothing and warned, "You'll freeze to death in a matter of minutes."

Brenya had already done the unspeakable. She was not about to let one small factor deter her. "The survivors must exist someplace warm. I'll find it."

The man edged as close as the door would allow. He showed her his face, his severity. He even modulated his voice as if to project concern. "Do you have any idea what they do to Omegas in Thólos? It is not a place you want to go."

Brenya met the striking blue of her prisoner's eyes. She held his gaze, knew *things* showed in her expression, and said, "It can't be different than what they do to Omegas in Bernard Dome."

"It is different, girl. You're not capable of understanding the savagery—"

She cut him off, "The first time, he ripped me open on the streets in broad daylight before a gathering crowd. I thought I was going to die... I almost did."

It seemed as if Jules had not heard that part of her story, if he'd heard anything about her at all. It was very subtle, but a change came over him. "You want that to happen to you again?"

"The people of Thólos need engineers to rebuild the Dome. If they want to survive, they will protect their best interests."

"You overestimate those animals. You wouldn't last a day."

Her attention went to the navigation panel at her left, Brenya focused and as abrupt as her companion. "I can't go back. After what I've done, he'll take one of your Omegas, a real Omega, and I'll be terminated. If I have to choose my graveyard, I choose Thólos.

I'm an engineering grunt. It's all I know, all I have ever wanted to do. I'll fix what I can. If the people of Thólos kill me for it, then at least I'll die doing something I love. How I die doesn't matter. Once I'm dead, I won't care who raped me or how much it hurt."

"Don't you believe in an afterlife?"

Her hand froze over the blinking map. "I'm not a Beta anymore. Their God would not have me."

"The Omega Goddess…"

He was wasting his breath, Brenya making her opinion clear in one harsh reply. "I'm not an Omega either."

The Beta flat out scoffed. "Then why do you smell like one who's about to enter estrous?"

VISION SWIMMING, Brenya blinked, wondering how it had grown hotter than the Sahara while she'd napped. Under her body the metal floor had imprinted its pattern onto her damp skin, just as the throb of a building headache had imprinted its tick on her brain.

With a groan she rolled to her back, instantly regretting moving. She was going to be sick.

Again…

There was already a pool of drying vomit in the

corner, the sour aroma doing nothing to make the boiling cockpit more comfortable.

"I would say you have less than an hour," the Beta droned from his side of the door. "Thirsty?"

Her mouth was a pit of sand, but all she could think of was the fountain in Beta Sector. How cool that water had been, and how awful the price she'd paid for tasting it. "I don't need a drink."

He rolled her a half empty bottle anyway. Before she could stop herself, she snatched it up and drained it dry. The momentary relief was short lived. Twisting her guts, a ferocious cramp left her curled into a ball of misery.

When it finally began to abate, another wave of nausea brought Brenya to her hands and knees.

"You may be farther along than I thought."

Throwing a hiss toward the door, she shouted, "Will you stop talking?"

"While you were resting, I took the liberty of following your example"—there were sounds of shuffling, the man raising from where he must have rested against the wall—"pulling wires, yanking out pipes. You should see the mess in here. Having seen you work, I doubt it would take you more than a day or two to repair. We'll be found before then."

"What?" Peering at her tormenter through lank, stringy hair, Brenya wailed, "No! Why would you do that?"

"Because the consequences of this ship even pointing in the direction of Thólos are further reaching than you know."

She wasn't listening, dragging her body to the console to confirm with horror that massive damage had been done. Sobbing, practically incoherent, she sank to her knees and hid her head in her hands. "I won't go back there."

Calm, rational, Jules said, "I gave you your chance to open the door, Brenya. There was no other way to prevent a massive international incident."

It was not the first time she had heard the stranger use her name. He'd been repeating it for hours since she'd cracked the door. *Brenya, open the door. Brenya, come closer. Brenya, drink.*

"Your Commodore is going to find this ship, if he hasn't already pinpointed our location with his web of satellites. It's inevitable." Fingers sneaking between the open crack, the Beta pushed forward, more intrusive than he had dared until that point. "The fact that you are moments from estrous might keep you alive. If he pair-bonds to you, he won't kill you. He won't be able to hurt you, not without causing great harm to himself."

She sunk to the floor to wail out her grief and decided she hated this male even more than all the others combined. "You told me to get out."

Another bottle of water was rolled until it hit her spine.

"You'll need to hydrate. Estrous is demanding on the body, and will be worse for you without assistance. Drink it all now while you still can."

She would rather swallow poison.

His monotone voice was grating on her ears, the Beta's incessant talking unbearable. Needing to retreat, to get away from everything, she crawled under the console. There was room enough to curl into a ball, enough shadow to feel a little safer, but there was no hiding from her failures.

If only the Beta had not been on the ship, she would have been free.

Low grunts hummed up the back of her throat with each exhale, a patterned cadence of female music peppered with whimpers as the pain returned full force.

With one mighty lurch everything inside her squeezed, a rush of fluid splattering her thighs to drip down and pool on the floor. Fingers between her legs, she tried to hold it in, only to find those digits playing in the slick and pumping inadequately into her body.

She had no control. "Nooooo."

The male, the one who had guaranteed her ruin, dropped his voice lower as if after all these hours, words had finally grown difficult. "You're okay."

"I am not fucking okay!" Even though her back was to him, she was masturbating in front of a stranger, unable to stop, and knew he could see. "Nothing about this is okay."

Those crystalline blue eyes were watching, focused, the entirety of his form filling up the small space the door would allow. "Listen to me, Brenya. I need you to hold one thought in your head. Whatever you do now, do not open the door."

"Open the door. Close the door. Make up your damn mind!" she shrieked at him, then whined when the worst feeling of emptiness flattened her to the ground. The Omega George had been fucking had made similar noises. She had twisted under him in search of relief.

At least that Omega had had a cock inside her.

No amount of furious rubbing of her clit, or fingering the place Jacques liked to taste, abated the need. Gods, it was awful. It scratched through her body, left her nipples on fire, her mouth drier than dust.

"Stop crawling this way." He looked as if he were straining to push through the small opening, even as he said, "You can't let me in there now. It's too late."

All she could think of was how much she wanted to be stretched until she squealed. She needed a knot, wanted to taste come splash her face and pour down her throat. The ground was so hard, the metal having grown slippery and unbearable.

Where was the softness, the cooling dark full of welcoming scents, and a strong male to bend her in half?

"Stay where you are, Brenya."

"I need..." Her eyes turned up, scalp prickling to find someone close enough to almost touch. "Make it stop."

The Beta took a deep breath, screwing his eyes shut. A single word left his lips on a whisper. *"Rebecca."*

And then he was gone, that sliver of space between the door and the wall as empty as her cunt.

25

I t was more than the pain.

There were no real words to describe the sense of emptiness—mind-numbing, hollow, torment didn't come close. It was like being injected with acid. Her every movement and wail completely out of her control.

Rational thought had fled hours ago.

One moment Brenya hallucinated she was still dangling upside down from the outside of the Dome. The next she was in the alley with Jacques while he ripped her apart.

When she asked him to stop, he dropped her, the ground falling out from under her to the point Brenya's skull bounced off the floor.

The blow woke her up.

She was back in the cockpit, where it was too

bright from sunlight streaming through the windscreen.

Or was it from the orange strobe emanating from the beeping console?

Hull breach. Or was that air regulation failure?

Or was that the sun glinting off the Dome as she was cooked alive in her bio-suit, abandoned by her people, and worthless without her assignment?

Another wave of cramping bowed her body off the ground, left her shaken… and blind.

Trying to blink through the spots, warbling hallucinations played before her eyes. A blue-eyed Beta kneeling, the front of his trousers soaked through with something offering the most delicious of scents.

Dragging her body across the floor no matter her creaking limbs, Brenya tried to reach the male. She would have too, missing the fact the Beta had been restrained, that there was a weapon pointed at his skull.

A pair of bio-suit boots stepped into her path.

They were scentless, just another obstacle between the only thing that might end this torment. Straining to reach through them, from Brenya's mouth came a series of incoherent filth that would have made an old whore blush.

The Beta was red-faced, eyes bulging. "Get me away from her!"

"If he so much as twitches backward, shoot him."

That voice… that was the baritone of another male, but she could smell only the one.

A boot heel came to her shoulder, pushing her spine to the floor. Broad form blocking out the horrible sun, the mechanics of the suit's speaker projected a soft question. "What am I to do with you, Brenya?"

Weeping, so close to relief but denied by the unshakable weight on her chest, she babbled, "Please."

"Is this an improvement over all I've offered? Here you are, in the very estrous I have been patiently waiting for, away from your nest, outside of the safety of our home, writhing on a dirty floor and so desperate for relief"—the figure pointed to the kneeling Beta—"you would beg for that to fuck you."

She'd given up trying to dislodge the boot, Brenya's fingers snaking down her belly to thrust themselves where the ache had only grown at the sound of that voice. Wet squishes were pointless music in air drenched with the song of female need.

In and out, pressure on her clit, nothing helped.

She needed a male, went back to staring at the only one, while spreading her legs wide so the Beta could see what was on offer.

It worked. The Ambassador was fixated on the show, struggling as if he too had a boot weighing down his chest.

"And now you know what it is to be Omega." The chuckle was coarse, muffled by the helmet electronics, and cruel. "It's my duty to drive that lesson in. Never again will you dare to defy me, *mon chou.* Never again will you put yourself at risk. I am Commodore, and I will protect the Dome and all who live in it. I will protect you from yourself."

The great form looming over her kneeled, pinning the female before she might scamper straight toward temptation. Jacques took her jaw, forced her head to face him, and shoved the padded fingers of his gloved hand straight into her cunt.

A sharp inhale, and the female fell back and spread wider.

"This should have taken place in a soft nest. For that, it's going to hurt more once I get my cock in you. I won't hold back, Brenya. Bad girls have to learn their place. By the time your estrous breaks, you'll have submitted to anything I demand. I'm going to take you in depraved ways that would make your sweet, virginal sensibilities recoil. Furthermore, you'll thank me, your Alpha. You'll beg me for more. You'll have no choice."

The thick bio-suit gloves abandoned her pussy and went to the reflective helmet's latch. As it lifted, the most enticing scent slipped forward to tease at the estrous high Omega's nose.

With a snarl, Brenya lost all interest in the Beta, reaching for that form holding her down as if salvation awaited.

One deep breath of her and Jacques grew vicious. He tore at the bio-suit, roared at her to spread.

But she was too far gone to pay attention. Tongue to salty flesh, clawing at any part that offered more perfect Alpha musk, Brenya rubbed herself against him.

It was not long before her back slammed against the wall with such force all breath was knocked from her body. Gasping, she was not even able to scream out her joy at the immaculate intrusion of an engorged, pulsating, and perfect cock.

One thrust, and the first knot was immediate. She had not even come, but her body began seizing in response to thick ropes of semen. Voice raw, Brenya's first scream caught in a sandpaper throat.

She needed so much more.

Laughing as she sobbed, the pain began to abate and hunger began to replace it. Legs wrapping tightly around the middle of a body that would make it all okay, she squirmed against the knot, and set her teeth to the nearest bit of flesh and broke skin.

A male roar shook her, but she would not let go.

Fingers wrapped around her neck, forcing her head back, and then a delicious mouth was on hers.

This was not pleasure; this was preservation.

She was already begging him for more, because the cramp had returned and his knot was not enough.

"*Mon chou*—"

Whining, tears running down dirty cheeks she pleaded, "Help me."

"You must be patient through the knot or I will not give you another one."

Sobbing against a sweat soaked chest, the inconsolable Omega mourned her short-lived relief. By the time he could rut again, she was far gone into another world of need, unaware of all around her but the insatiable frenzy to fuck.

Ruthless, just like he promised, he was rough with her—abusing her clit, tormenting her nipples, and coming at his leisure while pointedly denying her release by keeping the knot outside her body.

It took hours of her begging before he allowed her to climax properly.

The torture had done its work. Brenya was broken, sweating, twitching, and unable to follow even the simplest command.

"I think you've learned who owns your body, who can deny your pleasure, and who can take all your pain away." Jacques thrust in hard, rocking his pelvis exactly the way she needed, and lodging his growing knot deep in her core.

The scream wormed from her gut when her cunt began to milk him with ferocity, her hisses less animal and more maiden.

Lust drugged eyes blinked as if waking from a dream, an ocean of pleasure washing away consuming madness.

She knew that sculpted face, that golden hair. "Jacques?"

The little female was no match for the huge Alpha's wrath. "You'll never get away from me again."

The moment's clarity and the threat in his voice brought with it hysteria. Brenya tried to scramble out from under him, only for the Alpha to roar and flip her to her belly against the slick smeared, gritty floor.

When he forced his way back in, it felt so good, each punishing thrust drawing a wheezing scream from the female despite how she kicked her legs and refused.

It was not long before she was pushing her ass back against his hips, before she was squealing at the feel of his hand reaching under her to finger her clit. The beast grew appeased, less violent... almost gentle even when she submitted and climaxed when he ordered her to come.

Obedience was reward.

Growling with each breath, his weight on her back, a large hand began to rub the hair from her face. "Sweet girl."

Blinking, the *sweet girl's* eyes stared toward the cockpit door, toward the form of a tormented Beta who was openly ejaculating against the straining fabric over his erection as if it was his cock inside her.

There had not even been a form of friction to draw out his release.

He'd come from the sight and scent alone.

Their eyes met, even as Jacques began to pull her into another position. On her hands and knees with her breasts hanging down, the Alpha posed her as if taunting the Beta who wrenched against his restraints and strained to come forward.

It excited her, just as Jacques' massive knot excited her. There was no controlling the power of estrous or the total oblivion it brought to the mind.

Behind her, the Alpha knot began to fade, Brenya's body reacting exactly as it should have— pushing back against him, working his shaft to draw out another.

In front of the guards, in front of the Ambassador, her noises were that of an obedient Omega in heat. She even came crying out delight with a smile.

Her Alpha leaned his weight over her body, his

chest licking her spine. It was heaven, made all the better when he nipped a path across her neck.

"Dearest Brenya, punished and brought to heel. Give me your mouth, show them who you obey."

Tingles teased her spine into an arch, Brenya turning her head on command. He kissed her nicely for the first time since he'd begun, groaning, pleased when it was her tongue playing until the knot began to shrink.

The smile tugging at her cracked lips turned into a frown when instead of fucking her again, the Alpha pulled out.

Her scraped body was rolled to its back, and, though she resisted, her knees were pressed to her ears... but not so he might penetrate.

It was for inspection.

An endless dribble of semen and slick squished out faster the further he pushed back her legs. As she complained, a broad tongue passed over her slit, gathering up what spilled and sucking it into his mouth.

It was hers and she wanted it back, and tried in vain to push him off before he sucked out more.

When his mouth was full, he crept over her trembling belly, grunting in approval when she instinctively parted her lips so he might spill his catch into her mouth.

The sting in her throat grew soothed, hoarse

breaths softening as she swallowed. Over and over he filled her mouth, his fingers still toying with the flesh between her legs.

The more he touched her, the more he fed her, the more he fucked her... the more Jacques drew her deeper into his power.

It didn't matter that the filthy floor served as her nest—her estrous addled brain forgot to care who the Alpha was easing the need, that they had an audience... that she should have fought back with every fiber of her being.

The first time he coaxed her to sleep, some part of her felt Jacques still feasting on her breasts, fucking her dripping hole with smooth thrusts, and knotting at his leisure while she lay prone and too exhausted to move.

The moment she began to stir, he drew her to his lap, urging her to ride him while she leaned against his shoulder. Once she set a rhythm, he had a new show for the panting Beta at the door.

His fingers began to circle her anus.

It was pleasurable, the heat of his body, his touch, the purr—even the sound of his exasperation. "You risked the lives of millions, and for what? To get away from something we both know you enjoy? Badly done, Brenya."

Nosing his chest and ignoring his words, she yipped when a thick finger penetrated a place he had never breached before. When he added another, using her slick to pump smoothly in and out she raised her head and met deceitful eyes.

"Do you like that?

She didn't *dislike* it. Especially when he spread his fingers and made his wonderful cock feel all the bigger.

Jacques smiled. "You do…"

When another digit burrowed in, her eyes went wide, breath catching.

"The Dome is under immediate threat. As Commodore it is my sacred duty to protect it at all costs. I swore I'd keep you safe, and I will keep that vow." Jacques pressed a kiss to the distracted female's slack lips, playing with her ass while his gaze went to another. "Look at him, *mon chou*. He wants to fuck you; I can smell it. Even now he's watching my fingers and imagining they are his cock."

"More."

Throwing back his head, Jacques strained to keep from pounding upward and taking it all for himself when she begged so sweetly. "All these hours he's had to watch how perfect you are. All these hours he's had no relief. Even now he's trying to break out of his restraints."

Brenya, mindless of his words, moved her hips

with greater urgency—her ass burning, and her clit throbbing in time to his touch.

Voice shaking, Jacques removed his fingers and coldly ordered, "Release the Ambassador."

Loyal guards in bio-suits, impervious to the scent and show, obeyed.

There was no sound of a struggle, only the blow of a body crashing into the bouncing Omega. Before she might recognize that another male was pressing against her back, something much thicker than Jacques' fingers shoved full inside her second hole.

The Beta's manic thrusting upset her balance, Jacques' hands coming to her hips so he too might let loose his lust on the unknowing female.

Caught between them, stuffed in a way she'd never imagined, Brenya howled. The buildup of pleasure was instantaneous, washing over her with so many squeezing hands and so many nipping mouths.

She grew too full, but it was not the expanding knot, or the kick of a stranger's cock in her ass jettisoning Beta come—it was a river of energy shoving what she was out of the way—one that was pulling her under, sideways, and inside out.

When the bliss was perfect, sharp pain came to her shoulder, a stab of agony partnering the cruel bite when a second pair of teeth broke the skin of her neck.

Unwelcome sensation broke through her breast-bone, shattering her insides at the peak of debilitating orgasm. She was too weak to hold it back, the building chain that tore through her mind, her essence, her very soul, worse than the pair of males tearing her cunt and ass.

Choking as the world went black, the Omega was overtaken by an unthinkable distortion of self. The rage and lust rocking her body weren't hers... they were theirs—Alpha/Beta infections, and she could not shut them out any more than she could squeeze their sperm from the cavities they'd abused.

Jacques' final punishment had taken hold—a desecration of the pair-bond he'd sworn would bring her joy. She was not just tied to one. She was tied to two. And they were both completely rapacious, snapping up every last part of her until there was nothing left.

Thank you for reading STOLEN. Shepherd and Claire's story is far from over. Now, please enjoy an extended excerpt of CORRUPTED...

CORRUPTED
Alpha's Claim, Book Five

A wakening to the most glorious feelings of delight, Brenya smiled, nestling closer to what made the world perfect and new. Warm and protected, surrounded in scent, everything was delightful.

Fingers tripped down her spine, a satiny purr moving through her.

Fulfillment, conquest. Triumphant emotions stronger than any she'd ever known brought a satisfied flush to her cheeks and made her hum.

Until she realized they weren't hers.

Sucking in air as if suddenly drowning, finding her body was not floating, but actually in a great deal of discomfort, Brenya mentally flailed in the river of another person's emotions.

"Shhhhhh."

It hit her stronger, the alien sentiment, it swept her panic aside as if her own much weaker feelings were meaningless.

"Don't fight it."

A forceful psyche prevailed.

Jacques.

Finding herself back in his rooms, in his bed, naked, was shock enough to stop the heart. Realizing none of those wonderful feelings had been real, broke it.

This was not right. She was supposed to be free. She'd gotten out, flown a craft. Why was she not in Thólos repairing their Dome?

Someone was inside her skin, and though she held her fingers up before her face and found she could control them, the invasion was there all the same.

"Take a deep breath." Jacques' hand came to her chest. When she obeyed, he added, "Good, now take another."

Calm, he was inundating her body with manipulative calm.

Brenya's next blink led to warm drips marking her temples. Staring up in horror, she whispered, "What have you done to me?"

Leaning over, his golden hair loose and spilling around her face, Jacques smiled. Brushing his lips over her eyes, he kissed away her tears. "Made you mine, Brenya. You're mine completely now. My pair-bonded mate."

Estrous, the ship, bottles of water rolling over the floor... the Beta warning her not to open the door.

Hours of unbearable pain...

The memories were foggy with only flashes she might piece together, but a thrusting body had been on top of her. Someone had saved her from the pit of hell. Or had they dragged her to it? "It was you..."

"I was only a few hours behind you." Some of the Alpha's triumph was replaced with dangerous resentment. "You would have never made it, you know. That vessel was no match for the speed of my ship. I have an army of Alphas conditioned to throw themselves to their deaths on my order. Not a single one even questioned a mission that drew them from the safety of the Dome. I would have invaded Thólos myself if I'd had to."

And some of those Alphas had watched what she was beginning to remember. Shame formed in the pit of her stomach at the flashes of soldiers clad in bio-suits guarding the cockpit door.

Another with unnaturally vibrant blue eyes licking his lips as she moaned her release.

Cold, Brenya tried to turn to her side to shiver against the mattress. Jacques allowed it, settling against her back to toy with her hair and continue his internal gloating.

"I sense your dissatisfaction." Amazed, he scoffed at the back of her head. "You mistakenly believe that I will hurt you. I can practically read your thoughts, naughty girl."

This was a nightmare beyond comprehension,

Brenya whispering, "Don't."

"And now you're scared, worried, lost—internally reaching out for your mate to comfort your fears. As you should." He rewarded her by forgetting his anger and filling her with his joy. "I never want you to feel afraid of me."

His manipulation was so outright, she could hardly resist.

"You don't believe me," he spoke what he sensed, even daring to sound surprised.

How could she? Tears fell in earnest as the truth sank in. "You're going to kill George."

"No, *mon chou.*" His denial was echoed with raw internal confirmation. "The Beta is meaningless at this point."

Daring to glance over her shoulder despite a shooting pain that followed, she gave him a pathetic, "No?"

He kissed her red nose and smiled. "Don't cry. I don't want you to fear that there will be any retaliation for your recent... *hormonal behavior.* You were punished and are forgiven."

She was humiliated. She was tired. And she was guilty of much more than *hormonal behavior.* "What's going to happen to me?"

The arm around her middle tightened as Jacques pulled her flush to his body. "I'm going to make you feel better."

"I'm sore."

Husky, he chuckled, "I don't doubt it. In estrous you were a very greedy girl."

Estrous had been awful, and had left her wasted, body and soul. She never wanted to think about it again, any of it.

Jacques was not going to allow that.

"You were glorious through all of it, even when you refused to behave. It was the necessary choice to make, and had I not loved you so much, I never could have abided sharing... but it *was* exciting watching you take us both at once. Feeling another inside you next to me, hearing you come undone." Rubbing his thickening cock between the cheeks of her ass, he whispered, "I came harder than I ever have before... and Gods, so did you."

Jacques was against her back now, mirroring the motion. Brenya knew he'd planned his assault in such a way so she would have tactile memory of the Ambassador grunting at her ear.

There was no way to describe the sensations. Even allowing a moment of recollection sent an unwanted tingle and a small dribble of slick to gather at her slit. "It was wrong."

Tongue slipping out to tease the shell of her ear, Jacques teased, "Far from wrong. I know what's best for my rebellious, naughty Omega."

The Commodore rolled his hips as if to penetrate what was his.

Brenya angled away.

In answer to her unspoken rejection, the male caught her hip, purring, "Just as this will make you feel better," while thrusting slowly in.

Exhaling in an effort to handle the unusual discomfort of the stretch, Brenya found she had no will left to fight, that her body was weak, and that it did feel good no matter how much she wished it did not.

"That's right. I can make my defiant Omega sweet as cream." He took her breast in his grip, withdrawing his cock, before easing deeper with the second controlled thrust. "Before you know it, you'll whisper how much you love me."

Closing her eyes because she could not close her ears, Brenya grew limp.

"That's right."

Her nipple distended, peaking under a rolling pinch, and with little more than a few minutes of slow fucking, she already began to feel the early flutters of climax.

Soft and easy, the ripple of her muscles drew out a growing knot. The Alpha's groaned reaction fed her pleasure, even if the muscles that clenched around him were tender, even if her heart was not in it.

His was. His heart was completely taken with her.

When it was done and his knot tied her to him, Jacques traced his finger over the gash on her shoulder, and let out a satisfied sigh. "Now that you are awake, I'm going to kiss every wound, wash every scratch. Don't be alarmed by what you see in the mirror. Claiming marks are supposed to scar. Like the rest of you, they are beautiful."

Absently, she reached up to touch her neck where she hurt the most. There was a bandage covering the place Brenya remembered a stranger's teeth taking hold. "What happened to the Ambassador?"

A warm palm flattened on her shoulder, wrapping aching flesh in reverent fingers. "Jules Havel is the right hand man to the terrorist who destroyed Thólos. That is who you kidnapped and thought to take there—*a real monster* who has murdered millions of people. If your stolen ship had made it as far as the southern continent, you would have started a war Bernard Dome cannot win. Everyone you know, your George included, would have died. Their regime is merciless."

That could not be true...

But it was true; she could feel the sincerity of such a statement. The knot shrank, and she turned to finally look at the man who had caught her in his trap, shamed her before his men, and shared her with a stranger.

The lingering marks of her attack still bruised his face. His arrogant playfulness was gone.

"Why did you let him…" Why had he ordered his soldiers to set such a man free and offered her body to him. Jacques had encouraged the Beta to fuck her, to bite her, to join in his fun. Why?

"Hush, now, Brenya. You misunderstand." He kissed her quickly, cuddling the repulsed female. "Please listen to me when I tell you that everything, every choice I made, was in your best interest."

She didn't want his games or misdirection, she wanted answers. "What happened to the Ambassador?"

"Can you not tell?"

"No." Growing horror brought fresh tears, because there was something whispering in her mind. Something about that moment on that ship that Jacques had manipulated her into. "No."

"He won't be able to hurt you. Ever. The pair-bond will prevent it."

It was too much. There was too much inside her, too much to bear. "What did you do, Jacques?"

"I put a rabid dog on a leash."

Read CORRUPTED now!

ADDISON CAIN

USA TODAY bestselling author and Amazon Top 25 bestselling author, Addison Cain's dark romance and smoldering paranormal suspense will leave you breathless.
Obsessed antiheroes, heroines who stand fierce, heart-wrenching forbidden love, and a hint of violence in a kiss awaits.

For the most current list of exciting titles by Addison Cain, please visit her website: addisoncain.com

facebook.com/AddisonlCain

bookbub.com/authors/addison-cain

goodreads.com/AddisonCain

amazon.com/Addison-Cain/e/B01E1LKWMY

ALSO BY ADDISON CAIN

Don't miss these exciting titles by Addison Cain!

Smoldering Standalones:

Swallow it Down

Strangeways

The Golden Line

Thirst

A Night by my Fire

The Alpha's Claim Series:

Born to be Bound

Born To Be Broken

Reborn

Stolen

Corrupted

Wren's Song Series:

Branded

Silenced

The Irdesi Empire Series:

Sigil

Sovereign

Cradle of Darkness Series:

Catacombs

Cathedral

The Relic

A Trick of the Light Duet:

A Taste of Shine

A Shot in the Dark

Historical Romance:

Dark Side of the Sun

Twisted Tales:

The White Queen

Immaculate

Omnibuses:

Shepherd (Alpha's Claim, Books 1-3)

A Court of Poison